PRINCE
OF SECRETS

BY

LUCY MONROE

MILLS
BOON®

First published in Great Britain 2013
by Mills & Boon, an imprint of Harlequin (UK) Limited.
Large Print edition 2013
Harlequin (UK) Limited, Eton House,
18-24 Paradise Road, Richmond, Surrey TW9 1SR

© Lucy Monroe 2013

ISBN: 978 0 263 23240 0

Harlequin (UK) policy is to use papers that are natural,
renewable and recyclable products and made from
wood grown in sustainable forests. The logging and
manufacturing process conform to the legal environmental
regulations of the country of origin.

Printed and bound in Great Britain
by CPI Antony Rowe, Chippenham, Wiltshire

For Debbie, my sister and my friend.
God blessed our family immeasurably
when He brought you into it. And for Rob,
a dear brother of the heart. Together, you
have brought so much generosity, love, faith
and joy to our family and to me personally.
Much love to you both, now and always!

PROLOGUE

"WHAT AM I looking at?" Demyan asked his uncle, the King of Volyarus.

Spread before him on the behemoth antique executive desk, brought over with the first Hetman to be made Volyarussian king, was a series of photos. All were of a rather ordinary woman with untamed, curly, red hair. Her one arresting feature was storm-cloud gray eyes that revealed more emotion in each picture than he would allow himself to show in an entire year.

Fedir frowned at the pictures for several seconds before meeting Demyan's matching espresso-dark gaze.

Those who mistook Demyan for Fedir's biological son could be forgiven—the resemblance was that strong. But Demyan was the king's nephew and while he'd been raised in the palace as the "spare heir to the throne," three years older than his future king, he'd never once gotten it confused in his own mind.

Fedir cleared his throat as if the words he needed to utter were unpalatable to him. "That is Chanel Tanner."

"Tanner?" Demyan asked, the coincidence not lost on him.

"Yes."

The name was common enough, in the United States, anyway. There was no immediate reason for Demyan to assume she was related to Bartholomew Tanner, one of the original partners in Tanner Yurkovich.

Except the portrait of the Texas wildcatter hanging in the west hall of the palace bore a striking resemblance to the woman in the pictures. They shared the same curly red hair (though Bartholomew had worn it shorter), high forehead and angular jaw (though hers was more pleasingly feminine).

Her lips, unadorned by color or gloss, were a soft pink and bow-shaped. Bartholomew's were lost beneath the handlebar mustache he sported in the painting. While his eyes sparkled with life, hers were filled with seriousness and un-expected shadows.

Bartholomew Tanner had helped to found the company on which the current wealth of both Volyarus and the Yurkovich family empire had been built. At one time, he had owned a signifi-cant share in it as well.

"She looks like Baron Tanner." The oilman had been bequeathed a title by King Fedir's grandfather for his help in locating oil reserves and other mineral deposits on Volyarus.

Fedir nodded. "She's his great-great-grand-daughter and the last of his bloodline."

Relaxing back in his chair, Demyan cocked his brow in interest but waited for the king to continue rather than ask any questions.

"Her stepfather, Perry Saltzman, approached our office in Seattle about a job for his son." Another frown, which was unusual for the king, who was no more prone to emotional displays than Demyan. "Apparently, the boy is close to graduating university with honors in business."

"Why tell me? Maks is the glad-hander on stuff like this." His cousin was also adroit at turning down requests without causing diplomatic upset.

Demyan was not so patient. There were benefits to not being raised a Crown Prince.

"He is on his honeymoon." Fedir's words were true, but Demyan sensed there was more to it.

Otherwise, this could have waited. "He'll be back in a couple of weeks."

And if Mr. Saltzman was looking for a job for his son, why were there pictures of his stepdaughter all over the conference table?

"I don't want Maks to know about this."

"Why?"

"He will not agree to what needs to be done." Fedir ran his fingers through hair every bit as dark as Demyan's, no strands of gray in sight. "You know my son. He can be unexpectedly... recalcitrant."

For the first time in a very long while, Demyan had to admit, "You've lost me."

There was very little his cousin would not do for the country of his birth. He'd given up the woman he wanted rather than marry with little hope for an heir.

Fedir stacked the pictures together, leaving a

candid shot on top that showed Chanel smiling. "In 1952, when Bart Tanner agreed to help my grandfather find oil on or around the Volyarussian islands, he accepted a twenty-percent share in the company in exchange for his efforts and provision of expertise, a fully trained crew and all the drilling equipment."

"I am aware." All Volyarussian children were taught their history.

How Volyarus had been founded by one of Ukraine's last Hetmans, who had purchased the chain of uninhabited and, most believed, uninhabitable islands with his own personal wealth from Canada. He and a group of peasants and nobles had founded Volyarus, literally meaning free from Russia, because they'd believed it was only a matter of time before Ukraine fell under Russian rule completely.

They had been right. Ukraine was its own country again, but more people spoke Russian there than their native tongue. They had spent too many years under the thumb of the USSR.

Hetman Maksim Ivan Yurkovich the First had poured his wealth into the country and become its de facto monarch. By the time his son was crowned King of Volyarus, the House of Yurkovich's monarchy was firmly in place.

However, the decades that followed were not all good ones for the small country, and the wealth of its people had begun to decline, until even the Royal House was feeling the pinch.

Enter wildcatter and shrewd businessman Bartholomew Tanner.

"He died still owning those shares." Fedir's frown had turned to an all-out scowl.

Shock coursed through Demyan. "No."

"Oh, yes." King Fedir rose and paced the room, only to stop in front of the large plate glass window with a view of the capital city. "The original plan was for his daughter to marry my grandfather's youngest son."

"Great-Uncle Chekov?"

"Yes."

"But…" Demyan let his voice trail off, nothing really to say.

Duke Chekov had been a bachelor, but it wasn't because Tanner's daughter broke his heart. The man had been gay and lived out his years overseeing most of Volyarus's mining interests with a valet who was a lot more than a servant.

In the 1950s, that had been his only option for happiness.

Times had changed, but some things remained static. Duty to family and country was one of them.

King Fedir shrugged. "It did not matter. The match was set."

"But they never married."

"She eloped with one of the oilmen."

That would have been high scandal in the '50s.

"But I thought Baron Tanner left the shares to the people of Volyarus."

"It was a pretty fabrication created by my grandfather."

"The earnings on that twenty percent of shares have been used to build roads, fund schools… *Damn*."

"Exactly. To repay the funds with interest to Chanel Tanner would seriously jeopardize our country's financial stability in the best of times."

And the current economic climes would never be described as that.

"She has no idea of her legacy, does she?" If she did, Perry Saltzman wouldn't bother to ask for a job for his son—he'd be suing Volyarus for

hundreds of millions. As one of the few countries in the world that did not operate in any
sort of deficit, that kind of payout could literally
break the Volyarussian bank.

"What's the plan?"

"Marriage."

"How will that help?" Whoever she married
could make the same claims on their country's
resources.

"There was one caveat in Bartholomew's will.
If any issue of his ever married into the Volyarussian royal family, his twenty percent would re-
vert to the people less a sufficient annual income
to provide for his heir's well-being."

"That doesn't make any sense."

"It does if you know the rest of the story."

"What is it?"

"Tanner's daughter ended up jilted by her
lover, who was already married, making their
own hasty ceremony null."

"So, she still could have married Duke Chekov."

"She was pregnant with another man's child.
She'd caused a well-publicized scandal. He categorically refused."

"Tanner thought he would change Great-Uncle Chekov's mind?"

"Tanner thought *her* son might grow up to marry into our family and link the Tanner name with the Royal House of Yurkovich for all time."

"It already was, by business."

"That wasn't good enough." King Fedir sighed. "He wanted a family connection with his name intact, if possible."

"Family was important to him."

"Yes. He never spoke to his daughter again, but he provided for her financially until she remarried, with only one caveat."

"Her son keep the Tanner name." It made sense.

"Exactly."

"And he presumably had a son."

"Only one."

"Chanel's father, but you said she was the only living Tanner of Bart's line."

"She is. Both her grandfather and father died from dangerous chemical inhalation after a lab accident."

"They were scientists?"

"Chemists, just like Chanel. Although they

worked on their own grants. She's a research assistant."

The woman with the wild red hair in the pictures was a science geek?

"And no one in the family was aware of their claim to Tanner's shares?"

"No. He meant to leave them to the people of Volyarus. He told my grandfather that was his intention."

"But he didn't do it."

"He was a wildcatter. It's a dangerous profession. He died when his grandson was still a young boy."

"And?"

"And my grandfather provided for the education expense of every child in that line since."

"There haven't been that many."

"No."

"Including Chanel?"

"Yes. The full ride and living expenses scholarship she received is apparently what gave Perry Saltzman the idea to approach Yurkovich Tanner and trade on a connection more than half a century old."

"What do you want me to do? Find her a Volyarussian husband?"

"He has to be from the Yurkovich line."

"Your son is already married."

"You are not."

Neither was Demyan's younger brother, but he doubted Fedir considered that fact important. Demyan was the one who had been raised as "spare to the throne," almost a son to the monarch. "You want me to marry her."

"For the good of Volyarus, yes. It need not be a permanent marriage. The will makes no stipulations on that score."

Demyan did not reply immediately. For the first time in more years than he could remember, his mind was blank with shock.

"Think, Demyan. You and I both know the healthy economy of Volyarus sits on a precarious edge, just like the rest of the world's. The calamity that would befall us were we to be forced to distribute the funds to Miss Tanner would be great."

"You are being melodramatic. There's no guarantee Maksim the First's duplicity would ever be discovered."

"It's only a matter of time, particularly with a man like Perry Saltzman in the picture. His kind can sniff out wealth and connections with the efficiency of ferrets."

"So, we deny the claim. Our court resources far exceed this young woman's."

"I think not. There are three countries that would be very happy to lay claim to Volyarus as a territory, and the United States is one of them."

"You believe they would use the unclaimed shares as a way to get their hands on a part of Volyarus."

"Why not?"

Why not, indeed. King Fedir would and, come to it, Demyan wouldn't hesitate to exploit such a politically expedient turn of events himself.

"So I marry her, gain control of the shares and dump her?" he asked, more to clarify what his uncle was thinking than to enumerate his own plans.

He would marry one day. Why not the heir to Bartholomew Tanner? If she was as much a friend to Volyarus as her grandfather had been, they might well make an acceptable life together.

"If she turns out to be anything like her grasping stepfather, yes," Fedir answered. "On the other hand, she may well be someone you could comfortably live with."

The king didn't look like he believed his own words.

Frankly, Demyan wasn't sure he did, either, but his future was clear. His duty to his country and the well-being of his family left only one course of action open to him.

Seduce and marry the unpolished scientist.

CHAPTER ONE

DEMYAN SLID THE black-rimmed nonprescription glasses on before pushing open the door to the lab building. The glasses had been his uncle's idea, along with the gray Armani cardigan Demyan wore over his untucked dress shirt—no tie. The jeans he wore to complete the "geeky corporate guy" attire were his own idea and surprisingly comfortable.

He'd never owned a pair. He'd had the need to set the right example for his younger cousin, Crown Prince to Volyarus, drummed into Demyan from his earliest memory.

He'd done his best, but they were two very different men.

Maksim was a corporate shark, but he was also an adept politician. Demyan left politics to the diplomats.

For now, though, he would tone down his

fierce personality with clothes and a demeanor that would not send his prey running.

He knocked perfunctorily on the door before entering the lab where Chanel Tanner worked. The room was empty but for the single woman working through her lunch hour as usual, according to his investigator's report.

Sitting at a computer in the far corner, she typed in quick bursts between reading one of the many volumes spread open on the cluttered desktop.

"Hello." He pitched his voice low, not wanting to startle her.

No need to worry on that score. She simply waved her hand toward him, not even bothering to turn around. "Leave it on the bench by the door."

"Leave what, precisely?" he asked, amused in spite of himself by her demeanor.

"The package. Do you really need to know what's in it? No one else ever asks," she grumbled as she scribbled something down.

"I do not have a package. What I do have is an appointment."

Her head snapped up, red curly hair flying as

she spun her chair to face him. "What? Who? You're Mr. Zaretsky?"

He nodded, impressed by the perfect pronunciation of his name.

"You aren't expected for another half an hour." She jumped to her feet, the pocket of her lab coat catching the edge of a book and knocking it to the floor. "And you're going to be late. Corporate types interested in funding our research always are."

"And yet I am early." He crossed the room and picked up the book to hand to her.

Taking it, she frowned, her small nose scrunching rather charmingly. "I noticed."

"Eventually, yes."

Pink stained her cheeks, almost washing out the light dusting of freckles. "I thought you were the delivery guy. He flirts. I don't like it, so I ignore him if at all possible."

The woman was twenty-nine years old and could count the number of dates she'd had in the past year on less than the fingers of one hand. Demyan would think she might welcome flirting.

He did not say that, of course. He gave her the

smile he used on women he wanted to bed. "You have no filter, do you?"

"Are *you* flirting with me?" she demanded, her gray eyes widening in shock.

"I might be." Awkward and this woman were on very friendly speaking terms.

Her brows furrowed and she looked at him with evident confusion. "But why?"

"Why not?"

"I'm hospitably inept, not desperate."

"You believe you are inept?"

"Everyone believes I'm *socially awkward,* particularly my family. Since not one of them has trouble making friends and maintaining a busy social life, I bow to their superior knowledge in the area."

"I think you are charming." Demyan shocked himself with the knowledge that he spoke the truth.

An even bigger but not unwelcome surprise was that he found the geeky scientist unexpectedly attractive. She wasn't his usual cover model companion, but he would like very much if she would take off her lab coat and give him the opportunity to see her full figure.

"Some people do at first, but it wears off." She sighed, looked dejected for a few short seconds before squaring her shoulders and setting her features into an expression no doubt meant to hide her thoughts. "It's all right. I'm used to it. I have my work and that's what is really important."

He'd learned that about her, along with a great deal else from the investigation he'd had performed on top of the dossier his uncle had provided. "You're passionate about your research."

"It's important."

"Yes, it is. That is why I am here."

The smile she bestowed on him was brilliant, her gray eyes lighting to silver. "It is. You're going to make it possible for us to extend the parameters of our current study."

"That is the plan." He'd determined that approaching her in the guise of a corporate investor was the quickest way to gain Chanel's favor.

He'd obviously been right.

"Why are you here?" she asked.

"I thought we'd been over that."

"Most corporations donate without sending someone to check our facility over."

"Are you offended Yurkovich Tanner did not opt to do so?"

"No, just confused."

"Oh?"

"How will you know if this is a good setup or not? I mean, even the most fly-by-night operation can make their lab look impressive to a layman."

"The University of Washington is hardly a fly-by-night operation."

"No, I know, but you know what I mean."

"You really have no filter, do you?"

"Um, no?"

"You as good as called me stupid."

"No." She shook her head for emphasis.

"The implication is there."

"No, it's not. No more than I consider myself stupid because I could stare at my car's engine from dawn to dusk and still not be able to tell you where the catalytic converter is."

"It's under the engine."

"Is it?"

"Point taken, but you knew your car exhaust system has one. Just as I know the rudimentary facts about lab research."

"I know about the catalytic converter because my mother's was stolen once. I guess it's a thing for young thugs to steal them and sell them for the precious metal. Mom was livid."

"As she had a right to be."

"I suppose, but getting a concealed weapons permit and storing a handgun in her Navigator's glove box was taking it about sixty million steps too far. It wasn't as if she was in the car when they stole the thing."

Demyan felt his lips twitching, the amusement rolling through him an unusual but not unwelcome reaction. "I am sure you are right."

"Is English your second language?"

"It is." But people rarely realized that. "I do not speak with an accent."

"You don't use a ton of contractions either."

"I prefer precise communication."

Her storm-cloud gaze narrowed in thought. "You're from Volyarus, aren't you?"

He felt his eyes widen in surprise. "Yes."

"Don't look so shocked. My great-great-grandfather helped discover the oil fields of Volyarus. Did you really think I wouldn't know that the Seattle office of Yurkovich Tanner is just a satellite? They paid for my university education. It was probably some long-ago agreement with Bartholomew Tanner."

She was a lot closer than was comfortable to the truth. "He was bequeathed the title of baron, which would make you a lady."

"I know that, but my mom doesn't." And from Chanel's tone, she didn't want the older woman finding out. "Besides, the title would only pass to me if I were direct in line with no older sibling."

"Do you have one?" he asked, knowing the answer but following the script of a stranger.

"No."

"So you are Dame Tanner, Lady Chanel, if you prefer."

Her lovely pink lips twisted with clear distaste. "I prefer just Chanel."

"Your mother is French?" he asked, continuing the script he'd carefully thought out beforehand.

Demyan was always fully prepared.

"No. She loves the Chanel label, though."

"She named you after a designer brand?" His investigators had not revealed that fact.

"It's no different than a parent naming their

child Mercedes, or something," Chanel replied defensively.

"Of course."

"She named me more aptly than she knew."

"Why do you say that?" he asked with genuine surprise and curiosity.

He would have thought it was the opposite.

"Mom loves her designers, but what she never realized was that Coco Chanel started her brand because she believed in casual elegance. She wore slacks when women simply did *not*. She believed beauty should be both effortless and comfortable."

"Did she?"

"Oh, yes. Mom is more of the 'beauty is pain' school of thought. She wishes I were, too, but well, you can see I'm not." Chanel indicated her lab coat over a simple pair of khaki slacks and a blue T-shirt.

The T-shirt might not be high fashion, but it clung to Chanel's figure in a way that revealed her unexpectedly generous curves. She wasn't overweight, but she wasn't rail thin either, and if her breasts were less than a C cup, he'd be surprised.

That information had not been in her dossier, either.

"You're staring at my breasts."

"I apologize."

"Okay." She sighed. "I'm not offended, but I'm not used to it. My lab coat isn't exactly revealing and the men around here, well, they stare at my data more than me."

"Foolish men."

"If you say so."

"I do."

"You're flirting again."

"Are you going to try to ignore me like the delivery man?"

"Am I going to see you again to ignore you?"

"Oh, you will definitely see me again."

As hard as Chanel found it to believe, the gorgeous corporate guy had meant exactly what he said. And not in a business capacity.

He wanted to see *her* again. She hadn't given him her number, but he'd called to invite her to dinner. Which meant he'd gone to the effort to get it. Strange.

And sort of flattering.

Then he'd taken her to an independent film she'd mentioned wanting to see.

Chanel didn't date. She was too awkward, her filters tuned wrong for normal conversation. Even other scientists found her wearing in a social setting.

Only, Demyan didn't seem to care. He never got annoyed with her.

He didn't get offended when she said something she shouldn't have. He didn't shush her in front of others, or try to cut off her curious questioning of their waiter on his reasoning behind recommending certain meals over others.

It was so different than being out with her family that Chanel found her own awareness of her personal failings diminishing with each hour she spent in Demyan's company.

She'd never laughed so much in the company of another person who wasn't a scientist. Had never felt so comfortable in a social setting with *anyone.*

Tonight they were going to a dinner lecture: *Symmetry Relationships and the Theory of Point and Space Groups.* She'd been wanting to hear this particular visiting lecturer from MIT for a while, but the outing had not been her idea.

Demyan had secured hard-to-come-by tickets for the exclusive gathering and invited her.

She'd been only too happy to accept, and not just because of the lecture. If he'd invited her to one of the charity galas her mother enjoyed so much, Chanel would have said yes, too.

In Demyan's company, even she might have a good time at one of those.

Standing in front of the full-length mirror her mother had insisted Chanel needed as part of her bedroom decor, she surveyed her image critically.

Chanel didn't love designer fashion and rarely dressed up, but no way could she have been raised by her mother and *not* know how to put the glad rags on.

Tonight, she'd gone to a little more effort than on her previous two dates with Demyan. Chanel had felt the first two outings were flukes, anomalies in her life she refused to allow herself to get too excited over.

After all, he would get that glazed look at some point during the evening and then not call again. Everyone did. Only, Demyan hadn't and he had—called, that is.

And maybe, just maybe, she and the corporate geek had a chance at something more than the connection of two bouncing protons.

He understood what she was talking about and spoke in a language she got. Not like most people. It was the most amazing thing.

And she wanted him. Maybe it was being twenty-nine or something, but her body overheated in his presence big-time.

She'd decided that even if their relationship didn't have a future, she wanted it to have everything she could get out of it in the present.

Both her mother and stepfather had made it clear they thought Chanel's chance of finding a lifelong love were about as good as her department getting better funding than the Huskies football program.

Nil.

Deep inside, Chanel was sure they were right. She was too much like her father—and hadn't Beatrice said she'd married him only because she was pregnant with Chanel?

Chanel wasn't trapping anyone into marriage,

but she wouldn't mind tripping Demyan into her too-empty bed.

With that in mind, she'd pulled out the stops when dressing for their dinner tonight. Her dress was a hand-me-down Vera Wang from her mother.

It hadn't looked right on the more petite woman's figure, but the green silk was surprisingly flattering to Chanel's five feet seven inches.

The bodice clung to her somewhat generous breasts, while the draping accentuated her waist and the line of her long legs.

It wasn't slutty by any stretch, but it was sexy in a subtle way she trusted Demyan to pick up on. She would usually have worn it with sensible pumps that didn't add more than an inch to her height.

But not tonight. Demyan was nearly six-and-a-half feet tall; he could deal more than adequately with a companion in three-inch heels.

Chanel had practiced wearing them on and off all day in the lab.

Her colleagues asked if she was doing research for a physics experiment. She'd ignored their teasing and curiosity for the chance to be certain of her ability to walk confidently in the heels.

And she'd discovered it *was* like riding a bike. Her body remembered the lessons her mom had insisted on in Chanel's younger years.

The doorbell rang and she rushed to answer it.

Demyan stood on the other side, his suit a step up from his usual attire on their dates, too.

He adjusted his glasses endearingly and smiled, his mahogany gaze warm on her. "You look beautiful."

Her hand went to the crazy red curls she rarely did much to tame. Tonight she'd used the full regimen of products her mother had given her on her last birthday, along with a lecture about not getting any younger and looking like a rag doll in public. "Thank you."

"Do we have time for a drink before we leave for the dinner?" he asked, even as he herded her back into the small apartment and closed the door behind him.

"Yes, of course." Heat climbed up her neck. "I don't keep alcohol on hand, though."

The look in his eyes could only be described

as predatory, but his words were innocuous enough. "Soda will do."

"Iced green tea?" she asked, feeling foolish.

Her mother often complained about the food and drink Chanel kept on hand, using her inadequacies as a hostess to justify the infrequent motherly visits.

Demyan's eyes narrowed as if he could read Chanel's thoughts. "Iced tea is fine."

"It's green tea," she reiterated. Why hadn't she at least bought soda, or something?

"Green tea is healthy."

"Lots of antioxidants," she agreed. "I drink it all the time."

He didn't ask if the caffeine kept her up, but then the man drank coffee with his meals and had gotten a large-size fully caffeinated Coca-Cola at the movie.

"I keep both caffeinated and decaf on hand," she offered anyway.

"I'll take the caffeine. I have a feeling we'll be up late tonight." The look he gave her was hot enough to melt magma.

Suddenly, it felt as if all the air had been sucked

out of her apartment's cheerfully decorated living room. "I'll just get our tea."

He moved, his hand landing on her bare arm. "Don't run from me."

"I'm not." How could two simple words come out sounding so breathless?

His hand slid up her arm and over and down again, each inch of travel leaving bursts of sensation along every nerve ending in its wake, landing proprietarily against the small of her back. "I like this dress."

"Thank you." Somehow she was getting closer to him, her feet moving of their own volition, no formed thought in her brain directing them.

"You're wearing makeup."

She nodded. No point in denying it.

"I didn't think you ever did."

"I stopped, except for special occasions, after I moved away from home."

"An odd form of rebellion."

"Not when you have a mother who insists on image perfection. I wore makeup from sixth grade on, the whole works."

"And you hated it."

"I did."

"Yet you are wearing it now." The hand not resting on her back came up to cup her nape. "For the visiting MIT professor?"

"No."

"I didn't think so." Then Demyan's head lowered, his mouth claiming hers with surprisingly confident kisses.

And she couldn't think at all.

Sparks of pleasure kindled where their lips met and exploded through her in a conflagration of delight. It was only a kiss. He was barely touching her, just holding her, really. And yet she felt like they were in the midst of making love.

Not that she'd actually done the deed, but she'd come close and it hadn't been anything as good or intimate as this single kiss. She'd been naked with a man and felt less sensation, less loss of control.

Small whimpers sounded and she realized they were coming from her. There was no room for embarrassment at the needy sounds. She wanted too desperately.

She'd read about this kind of passion, but thought it was something writers made up, like werewolves and sentient beings on Mars. She had always believed that this level of desire wasn't real.

Before meeting Demyan.

Before this kiss.

The hands on her became sensual manacles, their hold deliciously unbreakable. She didn't *want* to break it. Didn't want to take a single solitary step away from Demyan.

Their mouths moved together, his tongue barely touching hers in the most sensual kind of tasting. He used his hold on her nape to subtly guide her head into the position he wanted and she found it unbearably exciting to be mastered in this small way.

Demyan was one hundred percent in control of the kiss, and Chanel reveled in it with every single one of her sparking nerve centers.

The hand on her waist slid down to cup her bottom. He squeezed. The muscles along her inner walls spasmed with a need she'd never known to this intensity.

She'd been tempted to make love before, but never to the point of overcoming the promise she'd made to herself never to have sex—only to ever make love. In her mind, that had always meant being married and irrevocably committed to the man she shared her body with.

For the first time, she considered it could well mean giving her body to someone she loved.

Not that she loved Demyan. How could she? They barely knew each other.

The feelings inside her had to be lust, but they were stronger than anything she'd ever considered possible.

He kneaded her backside with a sensual assurance she could not hope to show. She tilted her pelvis toward him, needing something she wasn't ready to give a name to. Her hip brushed the unmistakable proof of his excitement; they moaned into one another's mouths, the sounds adding to the press of desire between them.

The knowledge he wanted her, too, poured through her like gasoline on the fire of her desire.

Her hands clutched at his crisp dress shirt as she rocked against him, wanting more, needing something only he could give her. He rocked back against her, the sounds coming from him too feral and sexy for the "normal corporate guy" he was on the outside.

The disparity so matched her own newly discovered sexual being inside the science geek, the connection she felt with him quadrupled in that moment.

Without warning, he tore his mouth from hers and stepped back, his breathing heavy, his eyes dark and glittery with need. "Now is not the time."

Her own vision hazy with passion, all that she saw in focus was his face, the expression there an odd mixture of confusion and primal sexual need that could not be mistaken.

Even by someone as socially inept as she was.

Why was he confused? Didn't he realize how much she wanted him, too?

"We don't have to go to the dinner." She stated the obvious.

CHAPTER TWO

"No. We will go." He took a deep breath, like he was trying to rein in the passion she so desperately wanted him to let loose.

On her.

What would it be like to be the center of the storm she could see swirling in his intent gaze?

Shivering, she knew with absolute certainty that was one query she wanted answered.

"Do not look at me like that," he ordered.

"Like what?"

"You want to be naked," he gritted out as if it was an accusation.

Though how could it be? With the erection pushing so insistently against his dinner trousers, there could be no question his body was on board with hers in the desire department.

More to the point, *she* wanted *him* naked, but she didn't have the moisture in her mouth to say so. She simply nodded a hazy agreement.

"No. We have the dinner. Sex…" He shook his head as if finding something difficult to comprehend. "Sex will come later."

"Please tell me you aren't into delayed gratification." She'd found her voice and cringed at how blunt she'd been, not to mention needy sounding. "It's just that I don't get a lot of gratification at all. I don't want to put it off."

She snapped her mouth shut, biting her lips from the inside to stop any more untoward words from escaping.

Instead of reassuring her that it would be perfectly okay to miss the lecture, and dinner, and anything else that stood between them and making love, he seemed amused by her words. Darn it.

Demyan's mouth curved slightly and the need in his eyes receded a little. "Rest assured when we make love, you will not feel in any way ungratified."

Chanel usually objected to the euphemism of lovemaking for what was essentially a physical act between two people. An act she had heretofore refused to indulge in completely. They weren't in love, so how could they make love?

Only, she found the words of objection stuck in her throat. In fact, she could do nothing but agree with his assertion. "I'm sure."

He might be something of a corporate geek, but his confidence in his sexual prowess was too ingrained not to be well based.

Demyan helped Chanel into her seat, his head still reeling from how quickly he'd lost control with her back at the apartment.

He'd very nearly taken her right there in the living room. No finesse. No seduction. Just raw, consuming, *needy* passion.

Demyan did not do consuming. He did not do need.

Raw exposure of desire was for other men. He didn't hold back, but he didn't lose control either. He was known for showing maximum restraint in the sexual realms, bringing his partners to levels of pleasure they showed great appreciation for.

He did not lose it over a simple kiss.

His tongue had barely penetrated Chanel's mouth. With two layers of clothing between them, their bodies had not been able to touch intimately. He'd still been so close to coming, he'd had to pull away before he shamed himself with a reaction he'd never even evinced in adolescence.

The plan had been to give *her* a small taste of passion before leaving the apartment, to flirt with Chanel in subtly sexual ways over dinner and then leave her after a make-out session that left her wanting more.

Gaining her acquiescence to a hasty marriage with the prenuptial agreement the royal family's lawyers had already drawn up required strict adherence to his carefully thought out strategy.

The plan was to keep her reason clouded by emotion, unfulfilled lust built into consuming desire being the primary element.

He didn't plan to consummate their relationship for another week, at least. He wanted her blinded by her own physical wants, ready to commit to him sexually and emotionally.

Instead, he felt like an untried boy gasping for the chance to feel up under her skirt.

"Are you okay?" Chanel asked, worry in her tone.

Shaking off the disturbing thoughts, he gave

her his most winning smile. "Of course. I am here with you, aren't I?"

"Don't say things like that." Her frown was far too serious for his liking.

"Why not, when they are true?"

"They don't *sound* true." There was too much knowing in her gray eyes for his comfort. "That smile you give me sometimes, it's just like a plastic mannequin."

How odd that she should claim to know the difference. No one doubted his sincerity.

A smile was a smile. Except when it wasn't. As he well knew but had not expected his less-than-socially-adept companion to. Taken aback, he sat down, noting as he did so the interested looks of their neighbors.

He turned the smile on them. "What do you say? Am I sincere?" he asked an older woman wearing something he was sure fit a lecture hall better than a formal dinner hosted in the Hilton ballroom.

Her returning smile was the besotted one he was used to getting from women. Even academics. "Very. Perhaps your companion can't help her insecurities. Women like us don't usually snag such lovely escorts."

Chanel made a small, almost wounded sound next to him.

Before he could respond to it, the short, rather round man beside the older woman puffed up like a rooster. "Is that meant to imply that I am not as imposing?"

The woman looked at her date, and the smile she gave him shone with the kind of emotion Demyan found incomprehensible. "No, you are not, and that's exactly the way I love you. I would not have married you nearly forty years ago and stayed this long otherwise."

Feathers suitably smoothed, the man relaxed again in his chair, even deigning to give a somewhat superior smile to Demyan before turning to his wife. "Love you, too, m'dear."

The older couple became obviously lost in a moment Demyan felt uncomfortable witnessing. He turned his attention to Chanel, only to find her frowning, her expression sad and troubled.

"What is it?"

"She's right. You don't belong with me."

"That is not what she said, Chanel." He put

his hand on the green-silk-clad thigh closest to him. "I would say there is great evidence to the contrary."

"What do you mean?"

He did not answer, but his expression was as meaningful as he could make it.

He could tell the exact moment all the tumblers clicked into place in Chanel's scientific brain.

Her eyes widened, color surging up her neck into her face. "That's just chemistry. A kiss hardly constitutes a claim."

On that, he could not agree. Loss of control or not, their kiss had been a definite claim-staking on his part. "I'm surprised a woman of your education would declare there was anything *mere* about chemistry."

"We're *here*."

"And?"

"And if the chemistry was so amazing, we wouldn't be."

He couldn't believe she'd said that. He'd damn near ruined a pair of Armani trousers because of the heat between them.

They were not back at her apartment making love for two important reasons only, and neither had a thing to do with how much he'd wanted what she offered so innocently.

Making love tonight wasn't according to plan. Even if it had been, Demyan would have changed the plan because he'd needed the distance from his passion.

He couldn't tell her that, though. Not even close. "I thought you wanted to hear this lecture."

"I did."

He let one brow quirk.

"I do," she admitted with the truculence of a child, made all the more charming because he was fairly certain she had not been a truculent child.

Just a very different one than her mother had expected her to be.

From everything he'd learned about her, both from the investigative dossier and herself, Chanel Tanner took after her father, not her mother. Not even a little. Mrs. Saltzman had clearly found that very trying when raising her daughter.

An hour later, Chanel looked up from the furious notes she'd been taking for the past twenty minutes on her smartphone. "I'm enjoying myself. Thank you."

A genuine smile creased his lips. "You're welcome."

He liked seeing her like this, enthusiastic, clearly in her element.

"Dr. Beers has made at least two points I hadn't considered before. They're definitely worth additional consideration and research." Chanel glowed with satisfaction Demyan found oddly enticing.

He liked this confident side of her.

Afterward, Demyan made sure she got the opportunity to talk to not only the visiting lecturer but also the head of the university department overseeing her lab's research.

Her boss, who had attended the dinner as well, kept shooting her accusing glances from across the ballroom.

Demyan observed, "The head of your research is not happy to see you here."

"He doesn't like any of his assistants to make connections outside the department." Chanel didn't sound particularly bothered by that fact.

"That is very shortsighted."

"He's a brilliant scientist, but petty as a human being." She shrugged. "I have no aspirations to run my own lab."

"Why not?"

"Too much politics involved." She looked almost guilty. "I like the science."

That sounded like what Demyan knew of her father. "Why the frown?"

"My mother and stepfather would be a lot happier if I had more ambition, or any at all, really."

"Yes?"

"When Yurkovich Tanner offered my schooling scholarship, they made it clear I could attend any school I wanted to."

This was not news to Demyan, but perhaps she would explain why she'd opted for a local state school when she'd had the brains, the grades and the SAT scores to attend MIT, or the like.

"You graduated from Washington State University."

"It was close to home. I didn't want to move away."

Pity. It might have done both Chanel and her

mother a world of good. "You were still looking for a relationship with your mother."

He understood that, though he'd never told another soul. His parents had given him up in everything but name, but he'd never cut ties completely with them.

He'd spent his angst-ridden teen years waiting for them to wake up and realize he was still their son. It hadn't happened and by the time he left to attend university in the States, he'd come to accept it never would.

"I think I still am," Chanel answered with a melancholy he did not like.

"You are very different people."

"I'm the odd one."

"You are not odd." Unique, but not in a bad way.

"I wasn't the daughter she wanted. My younger sister is the much-improved model."

"That's ridiculous. You are exactly as you should be."

"Sometimes even I think you're being sincere."

Once again, she'd startled him. Because she was right. In that moment, he'd been speaking nothing but the truth with no thought of his final agenda.

* * *

Chanel wasn't sure of the proper way to go about inviting a man up to her apartment for sex.

Demyan wasn't making it easy, either. She wasn't entirely sure, despite the kiss earlier, that he would accept. He'd been attentive over dinner, made sure she enjoyed herself to the fullest. She'd even caught him giving her that look, the one that said he wanted her.

Only, she got this strange sense that he was holding back.

And not for the same reason she was so uncertain about this whole sex thing. No way was Demyan a virgin.

She couldn't help it—no matter how much her body was clamoring for sexual congress with this man, there was still a part of her that insisted that *act* was supposed to be a special one. Not very scientific of her, she knew.

Everyone from her mother, who had given up on Chanel's nonexistent love life, to friends who could not comprehend her "romanticized view of sex," agreed on one thing. Chanel's virginity was just another sign of how she did not fit into the world around her.

But making love was supposed to be something more than two bodies finding physical release, she was sure of it.

Chanel had never wanted just sex. Wasn't sure what effect it would have on her sense of self if she indulged in it now.

Things looked different at twenty-nine than they had at nineteen, though.

She should be more relaxed about the prospect of casually sharing her body with another person. She wasn't.

If anything, the older she got the more important she realized each human connection she made was. Sex was *supposed* to be the ultimate act of intimacy.

She had to admit she'd never felt the bone-deep connection with the few men in her past that she'd felt in that single kiss with Demyan.

She wasn't stupid. She knew losing the two people in her life who had loved her unconditionally at the tender age of eight had made her reticent about opening up to others, particularly men.

Her father and grandfather.

Chanel's stepfather hadn't loved her at all,

never mind without limits. As for her mother, Chanel was twenty-nine and the jury was still out on that one.

Which, as an adult woman, had nothing to do with the question of if and how Chanel should offer her invitation to Demyan.

His car slid to a halt by the curb outside her apartment building. He cut the engine, reaching to unclip his belt in one smooth move.

Maybe she wouldn't have to figure it out, after all.

"You're coming up?"

"I will see you to your door."

"It's not necessary." She could have smacked herself. "I mean, only if you want to."

Oh, that was so much better.

One dark brow lifted as he pushed his door open. "Have I ever left you to see yourself inside?"

"It's only our third date." Hardly enough time to set a precedent in stone.

Her own words hit her with the force of a solid particle mass traveling beyond the speed of light. What was she thinking? *Sex with him when they'd barely spent more than a minute in each other's company?*

Still remembering the pleasure of his kiss earlier, her body screamed *yes* while her mind sounded a warning Klaxon of *nos.*

No closer to a verdict about how to handle the rest of the night, she stalled in frozen indecision.

Her door was opened and Demyan bent toward her in his too-darn-sexy dinner suit, his hand reaching toward her. "Are you coming?"

She fumbled with her seat belt, getting it unbuckled after the second try.

The knowing look in his dark eyes said he knew why she was so uncoordinated.

"Don't," she ordered.

The knowing glance turned into a smirk. "Don't?"

"You're smug," Chanel accused as she climbed from the car, eschewing the help of his hand.

Ignoring her attempt to keep her distance, he put his hand around her waist, tucking her body close to his as they approached her building. "I am delighted by your company."

Heat arced between them and, that quickly,

she remembered why after only three dates she was ready to break a lifetime habit of virginity.

"I'm still not sure why we're here."

"You live here?" Amusement laced his voice as he led her into the unsecured building.

The lack of a doorman was a bone of contention between Chanel and her mother. If the older woman had been concerned for her safety, Chanel might have considered moving, but the issue was in how it *looked* for her to live in an unpretentious, entirely suburbanite apartment complex.

"I do not like the fact that the entrance to your home is so accessible. This dark cove outside your door is not entirely secure, either," Demyan complained as he took her keys and unlocked the door.

She hadn't quite decided if the action was some throwback to old-world charm or simply indicative of his dominating nature when he ushered her inside.

They moved into the living room and he shut the door behind them. There was meaning in that, right? The shut door. If he'd wanted only to see her inside, he could have left her on the landing.

"Would you like a drink or something?" Like her?

Was she really going to do this? Chanel thought maybe she was.

"Not tonight." The words implied he planned to leave, but the way he stepped closer to her gave an entirely different meaning.

She didn't reply, his proximity stealing her breath just that fast. For the first time in her life, she began to understand *how* her mother, Beatrice, had ended up pregnant by a man so very different from herself.

Sex *was* a powerful force. "Body chemistry is so much more potent than I ever believed." She sounded every bit as bewildered as she felt.

"Because you have never felt it so strongly with someone else." There was no question mark at the end of *that* sentence.

Chanel would take umbrage at the certainty in his tone if Demyan didn't speak the absolute truth.

"I'm sure *you* have."

Something strange moved across his features. Surprise? Maybe confusion. "No."

"You stopped earlier, not me."

"It was not easy."

Was that supposed to make her feel better about the fact he'd been more determined to go to the lecture than *she'd* been? Sarcasm infused her voice as she said, "I'm glad to hear that."

His eyes narrowed, a spark of irritation showing before it disappeared. She wasn't surprised. Demyan might not be the corporate shark her stepfather was, but he was not a man who liked to lose control, either.

Not that he had. Now, *or* earlier.

He had stopped after all, and right now, as much as she could read desire in his dark gaze, he wasn't acting on it.

She, on the other hand, was seconds away from kissing him silly. She, who had never initiated a kiss in her life.

"Do you want to stay?" she asked baldly.

Subtlety was all well and good for a woman who found the role of flirt comfortable, but that woman wasn't Chanel.

He smiled down at her. "Do you want me to?"

"I don't know."

Shock held his face immobile for the count of three seconds. *"You don't know?"*

She shook her head.

"You didn't seem unsure about what you wanted earlier tonight." Disbelief laced his voice.

She nodded, making no attempt to deny it. Subterfuge was not her thing. "I barely know you."

"Is that how it feels to you?"

She experienced that strange sense of disparity she'd had with him before. The words were right, the expression concurrent and yet, she felt the lack of sincerity.

Only, unlike at the dinner, there was a vein of honesty in his words that confused her.

"You already know you could take me to bed with very little effort."

"I assure you, the effort will not be minimal." Sensual promise vibrated in every word.

Chanel felt his promise to her very core and her thighs squeezed together in involuntary response, not because she feared what he wanted but because it made her ache with a need she'd never known.

"That's not what I meant." Her voice cracked on the last word, but she pretended not to notice.

The slight flaring of his nostrils and the way his eyes went just that much darker said he had, though. "What did you mean then, *little one?*"

"I'm hardly little." At five foot seven, she was above average in height for a woman.

"Do not avoid the question."

"I wasn't trying to." She'd just been trying to clarify, because that was familiar territory.

The rest of this? Was not.

Only he knew how tall she was, so if he wanted to call her *little one,* maybe that was okay. "I suppose I do seem kind of short to you. You're not exactly average height for a man in North America, though maybe I should be comparing you to Ukrainians, as that's your country's formative gene pool."

In fact, he was well above average height, certainly taller than most of the men in her life, and that gave her a peculiar kind of pleasure. Which, like many things she'd discovered since meeting him, surprised her about herself.

She'd never thought she would enjoy feeling *protected* when she was with a man, or that the difference in their height would even succeed in making her feel that way. Maybe it wasn't just that difference but something else about Demyan entirely.

Something intangible that didn't quite match his casual designer sweaters and dark-rimmed glasses.

"You do not seem *short*." He tugged at one of her red curls, a soft smile playing about his lips as if he could read her thoughts and was amused by them. "You are just right."

This time there was no conflict between the words and sincerity in his manner.

But it put the times there was in stark relief in her mind. "I can't make you out."

"What do you mean?" He looked surprised again and she got the definite impression that didn't happen a lot with him.

"Sometimes I think you mean everything you say, but then there are times, like at dinner tonight, when it seems like you're saying what you think I want to hear."

"I have not lied to you." Affront echoed through his tone.

"Haven't you?"

"No." Dead certainty, and then almost as if it was drawn from him without his permission, "I have not told you everything about myself."

"I didn't expect you to bring along an information dossier on our first date." Of course she didn't know everything about him; that was part of the dating process, wasn't it? "You don't know everything about me, either."

His gaze turned cold, almost ruthless. Then he adjusted his glasses and the look disappeared. "I know what I need to."

Sometimes there was a glimmer of another man there—a man that even a shark like Perry would swim from in a frantic effort to escape. Then Demyan would smile and the impression of that other man would dissipate.

CHAPTER THREE

DEMYAN DIDN'T SMILE now, but she knew the man in front of her wasn't a shark.

Not like the overcritical Perry, and definitely not like someone even more ruthless than her stepfather. There was too much kindness in Demyan, even if he was wholly unaware of it, as Chanel suspected he was.

"What did you mean earlier?" he asked, pulling her back to the original question.

Oh, yes…right.

"It's just…you must realize I'm a sure thing. Even if I'm not sure I *want* to be."

"Why aren't you sure?" he asked, deflecting himself this time.

Or maybe he just really wanted to know. Being the center of someone else's undivided attention when she wasn't discussing her work wasn't something Chanel was used to.

When she was with Demyan, he focused solely

on her, though, as if nothing was more important to him. He wanted to know things others reacted to with impatience, not interest. It was a heady feeling.

Even so, peeling away the layers to reveal her full self to him wasn't easy. "You'll laugh."

"Is it funny?"

"Not to me." Not even a little.

"Then I will not laugh."

"How can you be so perfect?"

"So long as I am perfect for you, that is all that matters."

"Do you mean that?"

"Yes." There could be no doubting the conviction in his tone or handsome features.

"Why?"

"Are you saying you feel differently?" he asked in a tone that implied he knew the answer.

"Love at first sight doesn't happen."

"Maybe for some people it does."

All the breath seemed to leave the room at his words. "Are you saying…" She had to clear her throat, suck in air and try again. "Are you saying you feel the same?"

"I want to be your perfect man."

"You mean that." And maybe it was past time she stopped doubting his sincerity.

How much of her feeling he was saying what she wanted to hear stemmed from her own insecurities? Why was it so hard for her to accept that this man didn't need her to be something or someone different to want to be with her?

The answer was the years spent in a family she simply didn't fit, the daughter of a mother and stepfather who found constant fault with a child too much like her own father for their comfort.

"I do."

She nodded, accepting. Believing. "I've never had sex."

Once again she'd managed to shock him. And this time she didn't have to look for subtle signs.

His whisker-shadowed jaw dropped and dark eyes widened comically. "You are twenty-nine."

"I'm not staring retirement in the face, or something." She had eleven more years of relatively safe childbearing, even.

Not that she thought she was going to marry and have children. She'd given up on that idea when she realized that even in the academic world, Chanel was a social misfit.

"No, I didn't mean that." But his voice was still laced with surprise and his superior brain was clearly *not* firing on all cylinders. "You're educated. *American.*"

"So?" What in the world did her PhD in chemistry have to do with her virginity?

"Are you completely innocent?"

Man, did he even realize how that sounded?

And people thought she was old-fashioned. "Even if I'd had sex, I would still be innocent. Sex isn't a crime."

"You know that is not what I was referring to."

"No, I know, but *innocent?* Come on."

The look he was giving her was way too familiar.

"I'm awkward," she excused with a barely stifled sigh. "I told you." Had he forgotten?

"You are refreshingly direct." That wasn't disappointment in his tone and the look she thought she recognized.

Well, it wasn't. He almost looked admiring. If she believed it, and hadn't she diced to do just that? "Mother calls it ridiculously blunt."

"Your mother does not see you as I do."

"I should hope not."

They both smiled at her small joke that did nothing to dissipate the emotional tension between them.

He put his big hands on her shoulders, his thumbs brushing along her collarbone, the hold possessive like before. And just like earlier, she found a new unexpected part of her that liked that. A lot.

"Demyan." His name just sighed out of her.

She didn't know what she meant by it. What she wanted from him.

He didn't appear similarly lost, his gaze direct and commanding. "You say you've never had sex. I want to know what that means."

It took two tries to get words past her suddenly constricted throat. "Why does it matter?"

"You can ask that?"

"Um, yes." Hadn't she just done?

"You are mine."

"Three dates," she reminded him.

"Love at first sight," he countered.

"You… I…"

"We are going to make love. What I want to know is what you have done to this point." His thumbs continued the sensual caress along her collarbone. "You are going to tell me."

"Bossy much?"

"Only in bed."

She wasn't sure she believed him, was even less sure if it mattered. She wasn't worried about standing up for herself. She'd never conformed when it counted, no matter how much easier it would have made her life—especially with her family.

Right now she found she wanted to answer his question, needed to. Still, she kept it general. "Heavy petting, I guess you'd say."

"Be more specific."

"No." Heat crawled up her neck.

He shouldn't care, should he? Virginity wasn't an issue for modern men. *Or modern women,* her inner voice mocked her, *and yet you are a virgin.*

He bent so close their lips almost touched. "Oh, yes."

Thoughts came and went, no words making it past her lips until she made a sound she'd never heard from her own vocal cords before. It was something like surrender, but more.

It was sexual.

The air between them grew heavy with the most primal kind of desire, pushing against her, demanding her acquiescence.

In a last-ditch desperate bid for space, she shut her eyes, but it did no good. She could feel his stare. Could feel his determination to get an answer.

She was super sensitive to his nearness, too, her body aching to press against his, her lips going soft in preparation for his kiss.

The kiss didn't come.

"Tell me," puffed across her lips.

The sound of his voice whispered through her, increasing the sensual fire burning through her veins.

"It wasn't anything."

"Were you naked?"

"Once."

"Good." He kissed her, his lips barely there and gone before she could lose herself in the caress she wanted more than air or research funding. "When?"

"In college."

He just waited.

"He told me he loved me." She'd wanted to be loved so badly, she realized later.

"You didn't let him into your body."

"No."

"Why?"

"It didn't feel right." Old pain twisted through her heart.

She turned her head away, stepping back when a few seconds before she would have said she wasn't capable of moving at all, much less away from him.

"He hurt you." The growl in Demyan's voice made Chanel's eyes snap open, her gaze searching for him, for visual proof of what had been in his tone.

The anger in his eyes wasn't directed at her, but it still made Chanel shiver. "He broke up with me."

Her ex had called her a dried-up relic, a throwback woman who belonged in a medieval nunnery, not a modern university. Chanel had a lot of experience with disappointing her family, so her ex-boyfriend's words should not have had the power to wound.

She should have been inured.

But they'd cut her deeply, traumatically so.

She'd never shared with another person the experience that had left her convinced her mother and stepfather were right, had never admitted her ultimate failure.

"I'm hopeless with men." What was she doing here, wanting to give her body to a man destined to eviscerate her heart?

He wasn't ever going to stay with her. He said they were going to make love, but they couldn't. He didn't love her, no matter what his words had implied. He couldn't.

She wasn't that woman.

Chanel wasn't a bubbly blonde beauty like her sister, Laura. She wasn't a cool sophisticate like her mother. Chanel was the awkward one who could make perfect marks in chemistry courses but utterly fail at the human kind.

She shook her head, her hands cold and shaking. "You should leave."

Another primal sound of anger came out of him before he crossed the small distance between them and yanked her body into his with tender ruthlessness. "I'm not going anywhere. Not tonight. Not ever."

"You can't make promises like that." His breaking them was going to destroy something inside her that her parents and ex had been unable to touch.

The belief that she was worth *something*.

"I can."

"What? You're going to marry me?" she demanded with pain-filled sarcasm.

"Yes."

She couldn't breathe, her vision going black around the edges. Words were torn from her, but they came out in barely a whisper. "You don't mean that."

He cupped the back of her head, forcing her gaze to meet his. "I do."

"You can't."

"I am a man of my word."

"Always?" she mocked, not believing.

No one kept all their promises. Especially not to her. Hadn't her father told her he'd always be there for her? But then he'd died. Her mother had promised, in the aftermath of Jacob Tanner's death, that she and Chanel would always be a team, that she wouldn't leave her daughter, wouldn't die like her husband.

Beatrice *hadn't* died, but she'd abandoned Chanel emotionally within a year of her marriage to Perry, making it clear from that point on that the only team was the Saltzmans'. Chanel Tanner had no place on it.

"Try me," Demyan demanded, no insecurity about the future in *his* words.

"You'll destroy me."

"No."

"Men like you…" Her words ran out as her heart twisted at the thought of never seeing him again.

"Know our own minds." There was that look in his eyes again.

As if he was a man who always got what he set out to, no matter what he had to do to get it. As if she might as well give in because he *never* would.

"I wanted to wait until I got married. I didn't want to trap someone into a lifetime they would only resent."

"There are such things as birth control."

"My mom was on the Pill when she got pregnant with me. I was not part of her future plans. Neither was my father."

"She didn't have to marry him."

"She loved him. At first." Chanel didn't know when that had changed.

She'd been only eight when her dad died, but she'd believed her parents loved each other deeply and forever. It was her mother's constant criticism and unfavorable comparisons later that made Chanel realize Beatrice had not approved of her husband any more than she did their daughter.

"They were not compatible." Demyan said it like he really knew—not that he could.

"I thought they were, when I was little. I was wrong," she admitted.

"We aren't them. We are compatible."

"You don't know that."

"I know more than you think I do. We belong together." There was a message in his words she couldn't quite decipher, but his dark gaze wasn't giving any hints.

"I told you I was a sure thing." Though she wasn't sure that was true. Part of her was still fighting the idea of total intimacy, especially at the cost of opening herself up like this. "You don't have to say these things."

"I am not a man who makes a habit of saying things I do not mean."

"You never lie." He'd as good as said so earlier.

Something passed across his handsome features. "I have not lied to you."

His implication was unbelievable. "You really plan to marry me. After three dates?"

"Yes." There was so much certainty, such deep conviction in that single word.

She could not doubt him, but it didn't make sense. Her scientific brain could not identify the components of the formula of their interaction that had led to this reaction.

In her lab she knew mixing one substance with another and adding heat, or cold, or simply agitation resulted in identifiable and documented results.

Love wasn't like that. There was nothing predictable about the male-female interaction, especially for her.

But one thing she knew—a man could not hide his true reaction to a woman in bed. It was why she'd refused her ex back at university. He hadn't been completely into it.

Oh, he'd wanted to get off, but she could tell

that it didn't matter it was *her* he was getting off with.

"Show me," she challenged Demyan now. "Make me believe."

His eyes narrowed, but he didn't pretend not to understand what she wanted.

Demyan could not let Chanel's challenge go unmet.

Whatever the cretin who had turned her off sex had done to her, at least part of her thought Demyan would do the same thing. He could see it in the wary depths of her gray eyes.

"You will see, *sérdeńko*. I am not that guy."

"You keep calling me little." She didn't sound as if she was complaining, just observing.

He noticed she did that when the emotions got too intense. She retreated behind the barrier of her analytical mind.

When this night was over there would be no barriers between them.

"You speak Ukrainian." Her dossier had mentioned she studied the language, but not how proficient she was.

To translate the endearment, which was a

diminutive form of heart, implied a far deeper knowledge of his native tongue than the investigative report had revealed.

"I studied it so I could read scientific texts by notable scientists in their native tongue."

"And *sérdeńko* came up in a scientific text?" he asked with disbelief.

"No." She sighed as if admitting a dark secret. "I like languages. I'm fluent in Ukrainian, Portuguese and German."

"So you could read scientific texts."

"Among other things." She blushed intriguingly.

"What things?" he asked, his mouth temptingly close to hers.

He wanted to kiss her. She wanted the kiss, too—there could be no doubt.

"Erotic romance."

"In Ukrainian?" he asked, utterly surprised for the third time that night.

This woman would never be a boring companion.

"Yes."

"I am amazed."

"Why?"

"If you like reading about sex so much, how are you still a virgin?"

"I like reading murder mysteries, too, but I haven't gone out and killed anybody."

He laughed, unable to remember the last time he'd been so entertained by a female companion.

This marriage he had to bring about would not be a hardship. Chanel Tanner would make a very amiable wife.

With that thought in mind, he took the first step in convincing her that they belonged together.

He kissed her, taking command of her mouth more gently than he might have before her revelation.

She couldn't know it, but her virginity was a gift to him in more ways than one.

First, that he was the only man who would ever share her body in this way was not something to take lightly. Not even in this modern age.

But second, and more important to his efforts on behalf of Volyarus, once Demyan had awakened her passions for the first time, Chanel would be more likely to accept his proposal of marriage.

It meant adjusting his schedule up for her seduction, but he wasn't leaving her tonight. Doing so might cause irreparable harm to the building of trust between them. She needed to know he wanted her, and he did.

Unlikely as he would have considered it, he desired this shy, bookish scientist above all other women.

She didn't want to believe in forever with him, but she would learn. He had spoken the truth earlier. Prince Demyan of Volyarus did not break his promises.

And he had promised King Fedir that Demyan would marry Chanel Tanner.

She whimpered against his lips, her sexual desire so close to the surface he thought she needed her first climax to come early so she could enjoy the lead-up to the next one.

With careful precision, he built the kiss until the small sounds of need were falling from her lips to his in a steady cascade. Control starting to slip, he deepened the kiss, wanting more of her taste, more of her response…more of everything Chanel had to give.

A small voice in the back of his mind prompted

that the time had come to pull back and lead her into the bedroom.

Only, his lips didn't want to obey, and for the first time in memory Demyan found himself lost in a kiss, his plans for a suave seduction cracking under the weight of his more primitive need.

He had just the presence of mind to move her backward toward the sofa. Unbelievably, *neither* of them was going to be able to stay vertical much longer.

Demyan maneuvered them both so Chanel sat sprawled across his lap, her dress hiked up, her naked thighs pressing against his cloth-covered ones.

He never let her lips slide so much as a centimeter away from his.

Demyan liked sex. According to Maks, he'd had more than his fair share of partners. Some of them were very experienced in the art of seduction, women who knew exactly how to use their bodies for maximum effect. None of them had turned him on as much as the uncalculated and wholly honest way Chanel responded to his kiss.

She moved with innocent need against him,

her body undulating in unconscious sensuality that drove him insane with the need to show her what those types of movements led to.

He brought his hand down and cupped her backside, guiding those untutored rolls of her hips into something that would give them both more pleasure and fan the flames of desire between them into an all-out inferno.

She jolted and moaned as her panty-clad apex rubbed over his trapped hard-on. He couldn't hold back his own sounds of raw sexual desire and keep from arching his hips to increase the friction.

The kiss went nuclear and he did nothing to stop it, demanding entrance into her mouth with his tongue and getting it without even a token resistance.

This woman did not play the coquette. Her honest passion was more exciting than any practiced seduction could be. She couldn't know, though; she was too unused to physical intimacy. For that ignorance, at least, he could be glad.

She could not take advantage of a weakness she did not recognize in him, and damned if he would point it out. He might not be able to control himself completely this first time with her, but no doubt that was a big part of the reason why.

It *was* her first time and he found that highly erotic.

The one benefit was that it was clear Chanel was completely out of control and definitely imprinting on him sexually.

Equally important, after what she'd revealed, was for her to realize *he* wanted *her.*

As she'd demanded, he would show her.

She would never again doubt her feminine appeal to him, not after tonight. And perhaps that, even more than her virginity, would lead her to accept his speed-record-breaking proposal when it came.

That it might no longer be completely about his duty to country was a thought he dismissed as unimportant.

He would have her. She would have him and whether she knew it or not, she needed him. He was good for her.

It started with now, giving her what she hadn't realized she was missing.

After insuring she kept the rhythm that made her body shake, he mapped her body with his hands through the soft green silk of her dress, caressing her in ways reserved for a lover.

He enjoyed this part of sex, touching a woman in ways no one else was allowed and, in Chanel's case, never had been.

Knowing a woman had put her body in his very-capable-to-dole-out-pleasure hands turned him on. Demyan liked *that* control, too. For reasons he didn't feel the need to dwell on, that knowledge was even more satisfying with Chanel than it had been with other women.

She might not realize it, but the kind of response she gave meant she would let him do *anything*. That acknowledgment came with a heady kind of enjoyment destined to undermine his self-control further if he wasn't very careful.

It was important for her pleasure, particularly this first time, that he not let that happen. He had to maintain some level of premeditation, or he could hurt her.

That reminder sobered him enough to think—at least a little—again.

Touching her was good, though. Too damn good.

He cupped her breasts, reveling in the catch of her breath as his thumbs brushed over turgid nipples. He wanted to feel them naked, but even this was incredible.

His sex pressed against the placket of his trousers in response to the feel of her in his hands.

He pinched, knowing the layers of silk and her bra would be no true barrier between those buds and the sensation he gave her.

She tore her mouth from his, her eyes opening, pupils blown with bliss almost swallowing the stormy irises. "I… That…"

"Is good." He did it again, increasing the pressure just enough to give maximum pleasure that might border on pain but would never go over. "Say it."

CHAPTER FOUR

CONFUSION FLITTED ACROSS the sweet oval of Chanel's face. "What?"

"Say it feels good."

She didn't have to speak her refusal—it was there in the way her body stiffened and she averted her gaze.

"Look at me," he demanded, his fingers poised to give more pleasure but not offering it. "Look at me and say it."

Her storm-cloud gaze came back to his, her mouth working, no words coming out.

"You are a woman. You can acknowledge your own pleasure, Chanel. I believe in you."

"It's not that." The word cut off as if her air had run out. She took a deep breath and let it out, her tongue coming out to wet her lips. "I know sex is supposed to feel good."

"Do you?"

"I've read books."

"Erotic books."

"Yes."

"So, say it."

"You want to strip me bare," she accused.

He saw no point in denying it. "Yes."

"Why?"

"You have to let go."

"You never let go."

"I am the experienced one here. If I let go of my control, we'd both be in trouble."

"That doesn't make sense."

"Only because you haven't done this before."

She didn't deny his words. "I like it."

"I know." He pressed just slightly, giving her a taste of what was to come.

She moaned, her head falling back, her eyelids sliding down to cover the vulnerability in her gaze. "So, why do I have to say it?"

"For me. Say it for me."

"It feels good." The words came out in a low, throaty whisper infused with sincerity.

Oh, yes, this woman would learn to hold nothing back.

He rewarded her with more pleasure until she

was rocking against him with gasping breaths. "Demyan!"

"What, *sérdeńko?*"

"You know! You have to know."

"This?" he asked as he pushed up to rub his hardness against her, pinching her nipples at the same time.

"Yes."

He did it again, making sure to continue the friction against that bundle of nerves through the damp silk of her panties. "Let go, Chanel."

"I…"

He didn't want arguments. He wanted her surrender. "Come for me, Chanel. You are mine."

And unused to this level of pleasure, she came apart, her body arching into a stiff contortion of delight while a keening wail sounded from her throat.

Oh, yes, this woman belonged to him. Her body knew it, even if her mind was still in some doubt.

He let the shivers of aftershock finish, concentrating on gaining his own breath and a measure of mental fortitude. When he was sure he could do it without his own limbs giving way, he tucked one arm under her bottom and the other against her back and stood with her secure in his hold.

Her head rose from where it had come to rest against his shoulder, her face still flushed with pleasure, her gray gaze meeting his. "What… Where?"

"Your first time will not happen on a sofa, no matter how comfortable."

"It already did."

He shook his head. "That was not sex."

"But it was my first orgasm with another person."

Perhaps that small fact helped to explain why she was still a virgin, too.

He didn't repeat his shock at her age, or his disgust with her previous partners. "It will be the first of many, I promise you."

She swallowed audibly, but nodded with appreciative enthusiasm.

He felt his mouth curve into a very rare and equally genuine smile.

How had she remained untouched so long?

This woman was sweetly sensual and engag-

ingly honest. Far from socially inept. Demyan
found her fascinating.

It did not bother him at all, though, that she
would be giving her body to him and only him.
He would honor the gift and she would find no
reason to regret it.

He made the vow to himself, and Demyan
never broke his word. Chanel was still trying
to catch her breath when Demyan laid her oh
so carefully on the bed after yanking back the
covers.

Sexual demand radiated off him like heat from
a nuclear reactor. Yet there was no impatience
in the way he handled her.

The bedding? Yes. It lay in disarray on the
floor, his powerful jerks pulling the sheet and
blanket that had been tucked between the mat-
tress and box spring completely away.

But her?

He settled with a gentle touch that belied his
obvious masculine need.

"I was going to wait." He shrugged out of his
suit jacket, letting the designer garment drop to
the floor without any outward concern about
what that might do to it.

"Why?"

"It seemed the thing to do."

"Because things are moving so fast between us," she said rather than asked.

He only loosened his tie and undid the top buttons on his shirt before pulling the whole thing over his head in one swift movement. "We will not be waiting."

His torso was chiseled in that way really fit men with natural strength were. Dark curls covered his chest, narrowing into a V that disappeared into the waistband of his trousers. She wanted to see where that trail of sexy hair led.

She might be a virgin, but she was pretty sure she wasn't a shy one.

"You are beautiful," she breathed.

"Men are not beautiful." But his eyes smiled at the compliment.

"The statue of David is beautiful."

"That is art."

"So are you."

He shook his head, his hands going to his trouser button. "I am a flesh-and-blood man, never doubt it."

How could she, with all that flesh staring her in the face?

His trousers slid down his legs, revealing CK black knit boxers that conformed to every ridge of muscle and the biggest ridge of all. His erection.

Her mouth went dry, the moisture going straight to her palms. "You're big, aren't you?"

"I've never compared myself to other men." With that he shucked out of his boxers, leaving his very swollen, very rigid length on display.

"According to scientific studies, the average penile length is five to five-point-seven inches in length when erect." And Demyan was definitely longer, unless her eyes were deceiving her.

But Chanel was a scientist who had conducted enough measurements she could usually guess within a centimeter's accuracy.

He frowned and stopped at the side of the bed, his erection bobbing with the movement even as it curved upward toward his belly. That wasn't usual, either, she'd read. Most men erected perpendicularly with a slight leaning toward one side. Some even had a small downward angle.

For Demyan's hardness to be curving upward, it had to be *extremely* ready for intercourse.

"How do you know that?" he demanded with amusement in his voice.

"I read. A lot."

"You cannot believe everything you read in your Ukrainian erotica."

"Of course not."

His brow rose, the mockery there.

"I read that particular fact in a scientific journal."

His dark gaze pinned her to the bed, though he had yet to join her with his incredibly gorgeous naked body. "We have better things to do than discuss frivolous scientific research."

"It isn't frivolous to the tens of thousands of men who have been feeling inadequate because of the supposed average lengths gleaned from self-measurement."

"What you are telling me is that men measure themselves as larger than they are?" He definitely sounded amused now.

"I don't think *you* would."

"I would not measure myself at all." From his

tone, he found the idea of doing so absolutely ridiculous.

"I think I'd like to measure you."

"No."

"With my hand."

The erection in question jumped at her words and it was her turn to smile.

"Do not tease," he warned.

"I'm not teasing."

"You are smiling."

"I'm just really happy that you react to me so strongly." So strongly in fact that despite the fact she'd led them down one of the conversational byways that always annoyed others, his visible response to her had not dimmed in the least.

"You are a very sexy woman."

She couldn't help laughing at that assertion, but she didn't accuse him of lying. Honest desire burned in the brown depths of his eyes.

"It is time I did something about your lack of focus." He didn't sound mad about it, though.

She just nodded, wanting more of what they'd done in the living room, more kisses, more touching, more of that amazingly intimate connection.

"First we need to get you naked, too."

She'd already kicked her heels off in the living room and she wasn't wearing panty hose. That didn't leave much to get rid of.

She started tugging her skirt up, only to have his hands join her in the effort. Only somehow he made the slide of silk up her body into a series of sensual caresses, so she was shivering with renewed passion by the time he pulled the green fabric over her head.

He tossed it away.

"My mother would be very annoyed if she saw you treating clothes the way you do." Especially high-end designer ones.

"Your mother has no place in our bedroom."

"It's not *our* bedroom."

"You belong to me. This room belongs to you. Therefore, it is ours."

She couldn't push a denial of his claim through her lips. There was too much truth to it.

It was almost scary, but she wasn't afraid.

In fact, that part of her that had felt alone in the world since her mother's marriage to Perry Saltzman warmed with an inexplicable sense of belonging.

"She's still my mother," was all Chanel could think to say.

"And she always will be, but her views and opinions about you are skewed by grief and a lack of understanding. Therefore, they have no place in our life together."

"We don't have a life together," she said with more vehemence than she felt.

But it was insane, this instant connection, his claim he planned a future with her. It just wasn't real. Couldn't be.

"We do. It starts with this." His hands reached behind her to unhook her bra clasp, sight unseen.

Her nipples, already tightened into hard points from his earlier manipulations, contracted further from the cooled air brushing across them.

There was no stifling the shiver that went through her in response to the extra stimulation.

His smile was predatory. "You have very sensitive breasts."

"Nipples," she couldn't help correcting. It wasn't her entire boob responding, was it?

He brushed his fingertips along the side of her breast, sliding forward, but not touching the nipple.

Desire coiled low in her belly, her body arching toward his.

He did it again. "Very responsive."

"You don't like to be wrong, do you?" she asked in a voice that hitched every other syllable with her gasping breaths.

"It is a rare occurrence."

"Arrogant."

"Certain."

"Same thing."

"It is not." Then he kissed her, preventing any more words.

It was a sneaky way to end an argument, but she couldn't make herself mind. Not when it felt so wonderful. It might be only their lips that were connected, but she felt as if he was touching her to the very depths of her soul.

He pulled back, their breath coming in harsh gasps between them. "One thing left."

"What?" she asked, nothing but his lips making any sense in that moment.

"Your panties."

Were surplus to requirements. She got the picture but found she was hopeless in the face of doing something about it.

It was okay, though. His long masculine fingers were sliding between her hips and the silk and then it was being tugged down, baring the last bit of her to him.

"There will be nothing between us," he growled, as if he could read her mind.

She looked up at him, their gazes locking, and what she saw in his left her in no doubt he *wasn't* just talking about clothing.

He'd pushed her in the living room, demanding she acknowledge her own pleasure, her own desires, this crazy thing happening between them.

He was going to push her further now.

"It's just sex," she claimed with a desperate attempt to believe her own words.

"We are making love, locking our lives together."

"This isn't real."

"It is very real."

"Please…"

He cupped her face, the move one she was becoming quite familiar with and incidentally learning to love. "Please, what?"

"Just tonight? Can it just be about tonight?"

He lowered his head until their lips almost brushed. "No."

This time, she kissed him. Couldn't help herself and was glad she hadn't when he took control and drew forth a response from her body that shouldn't have been possible. Not after she'd just climaxed.

Only it was.

It was as if they were connected by live electric current, energizing, transforming every synapse in its wake, so that her body was uniquely tuned to him. The way that big body blanketed hers, his hardness rubbing against the sensitive curls at the apex of her thighs indicated he was being tuned to the same frequency.

A frequency she thought would rule her body's responses for the rest of her life.

And if she could believe his words, it would.

The kiss pulled her out of time, suspending them in an intimacy that had no limits, not in hours and minutes, or in emotional connection.

It was beyond anything she thought two people could feel together.

His hands were everywhere, bringing pleasure, teaching her body his touch, making that indescribable pleasure spiral tighter and tighter inside her again.

She touched him, too, letting her fingertips learn his body, and just doing that gave her a level of delight she'd never known. She could caress this man, touch his naked skin and he wanted it, wanted *her* touch. Not just any woman's. *Hers.*

An empty ache started, making her body restless for what it had never known.

As if he knew exactly what she needed, he nudged her thighs apart and adjusted his body so the head of his erection pressed against the opening to her body. However, he made no move to enter her.

The moment felt so momentous that tears washed into her eyes and trickled down her temples. He broke the kiss, lifting his head, his expression knowing.

He touched the wetness, wiping at the tears with one finger. "It is not just about tonight."

"It's not supposed to be this big."

"You have waited twenty-nine years, *krýxitka.*"
She wasn't a baby, not by any stretch, but

having him call her one didn't feel wrong. "But women don't, anymore."

"You had your reasons."

"I want this."

"I know."

"You do, too."

"Yes."

"With *me*," she confirmed, maybe needing a little more reassurance than she'd realized.

"Only *you* from this point forward."

"You do not believe in infidelity?" A lot of businessmen thought it was their right when they flew out of town to leave their wedding ring in the bedside drawer of their hotel rooms.

Or so she'd read. Honestly, as awful as Perry might be toward Chanel, she couldn't imagine him cheating on her mother. It was one of the reasons she respected him, even if she didn't like the business shark.

She could never respect a man who didn't understand and adhere to the true meaning of loyalty and faithfulness.

"It is too damaging to everyone involved." There was something about Demyan's tone that said he knew exactly what he was talking about.

She would have asked about it, but right now all she could really focus on was how much she needed him inside her. "It's time."

"Not yet."

Unexpected anger welled up. "You're not going to get bossy about this. I'm not begging."

"I don't want you begging. Tonight."

"But—"

He smiled down at her, indulgence and tenderness she wasn't even sure he was aware of glowing in his dark gaze. "You are a virgin. A certain amount of preparation will make the difference between a beautiful experience and one you never want to have to remember."

"You make it sound so dire."

"It can be."

"Much experience deflowering virgins?" she asked with sarcasm and maybe just a hint of jealousy.

"Tonight is not the time for discussing past sexual encounters."

"That isn't what you said earlier."

His jaw hardened but he said, "Fine. She was young. I was young. It was a disaster."

"Did you love her?"

"Not even a little."

"Did she love you?"

"No." No doubt there.

"You decided to figure out how to fix the problem." She could so see him doing that.

She might not know everything there was to about this man, but some of his basic characteristics she understood very well.

He nodded even as he shifted again so there was room for his hand to get between them. A single finger gently rubbed along her wet folds.

"That feels good," she whispered.

"It is supposed to."

The touch moved up, circling her clitoris. It felt so delicious she gasped with the pleasure of it.

He kissed her and then lifted his head. "Touching you is such a pleasure. You hide none of your responses from me."

"Am I supposed to?"

"No." Very definite. Unquestionably vehement.

"You're kind of a control freak in bed, aren't you?"

"Giving you pleasure takes a lot of concentration. Why would you try to hinder my efforts by lying to me?"

"I never…" She gasped as his fingers moved a certain way. "Didn't say I would."

"Never?" he asked.

She could have accused him of taking unfair advantage, but really? It wouldn't have mattered if he'd asked her in the middle of the street standing ten feet away.

Her answer to that question would always be the same. "Never."

"Thank you." Demyan continued to touch her until she was moving restlessly beneath him.

"Please…" She wasn't even sure what she was asking for.

Intercourse? Maybe, but what she really wanted was resolution to the storm building inside her and Chanel didn't really care how she got it.

Even so, she was shocked when he shifted down her body, his intention clear. She'd read about this. Of course she had. Her ex-boyfriend had even wanted to do it to her, but he'd told her she'd have to shave her hair off first.

She'd refused.

Demyan didn't seem in the least put off by the damp curls between her legs, his tongue going with unerring accuracy right to where his finger had been.

She cried out, her hips coming off the bed. His mouth followed, his ministrations with lips and tongue never pausing.

This was oral sex? This intimate kiss that led to feeling so close to someone else that there was nothing embarrassing about it?

She always thought it would bother her to have a man's mouth *there*. She hadn't refused to shave her nether region just because she was a prude back then.

Only it didn't bother her. Not at all.

It felt so good, so perfect.

Demyan's fingers came back to play, this time with one of them sliding just inside her as his tongue swirled over her most sensitive spot. He moved the finger in and out, going a little deeper each time until he pressed gently against her body's barrier.

It didn't hurt; it was not too much pressure, but it would be different when he was inside her. Wouldn't it?

He would have to break through the barrier then. With his longer-than-average erection. That's what had to happen next.

Only, he didn't seem to have the script, because he kept licking, sucking and nibbling at her clitoris until she was on the verge of climax. His finger inside her continued sliding in and out of her channel, pressing just a little bit harder against the thin barrier every few times.

His other hand came up to play with her breasts and tease at her nipples, increasing the sensations below by a factor of ten. It was incredible. Amazing.

And she felt that precipice draw closer and closer. She didn't think she was supposed to climax again before they were joined, but she didn't worry about it. He knew what he was doing and wouldn't let her.

Only, he didn't seem concerned when she warned him it was getting to be too much. He only renewed his efforts, sucking harder on her clitoris and nipping it ever so gently with his teeth.

Without warning, her body splintered apart in glorious pleasure again, this time so intense she couldn't even get enough air to scream. He didn't stop the intimate kiss, but he gentled it, bringing her prolonged ecstasy that went on and on even as his finger pressed more insistently against that thin membrane of flesh inside.

Until, as she floated on a cloud of sensual bliss, she felt the sharp sting of pain and realized he'd broken through the barrier of her body. With his finger.

"What? Why?" she asked, the hazy peace cracking a little.

"It hurts less." He gently withdrew his finger before placing a single soft kiss against her nether lips.

It felt like a benediction.

He moved off her and she saw him grab a corner of the sheet from the floor to wipe his face and hand before he rejoined her on the bed.

Demyan pulled her body into his still-very-aroused one, his expression very satisfied. "You are beautiful in your passion, Chanel."

"We... Aren't you going to..."

"Oh, yes. But only when you are ready to begin building toward climax again."

She didn't know what he meant, but he showed

her, after cuddling her and telling her how amazing and lovely she was. After his touch and nearness once again began to draw forth need to be joined with him.

When he finally pressed inside her, she cried for the second time that night. He didn't look in the least worried he'd hurt her, though. In fact, his expression was one of understanding overlaying utter male satisfaction.

She didn't begrudge him one iota of it, either.

He might have had a debacle with his first virgin, but he'd made this one's initiation into intimacy unbelievably good.

Once she started to move against him, his control slipped its leash and his passion turned harsh and exciting. She screamed her pleasure this time even as his body pounded into hers, and his shout was loud enough to make her ears ring.

Afterward he was quiet, his expression impossible to read. "You'll want a shower."

"Couldn't we shower together?" she asked.

"Your bathroom isn't meant for shared intimacies."

She hadn't been propositioning him, couldn't

believe he thought she had any energy left for *that,* but she didn't say so.

While she was in the shower she tried to go over what had happened, but couldn't figure out why he'd withdrawn and wondered if he'd even still be there when she came out.

CHAPTER FIVE

HE WAS, THOUGH, and he'd remade the bed with fresh sheets.

"Thank you," she said, feeling unsure.

"We will be more comfortable sleeping on clean bedding."

That one small word washed through her like life-giving oxygen. *We.* He'd said *we.*

Before she could remark on it, or say anything at all, he started toward the bathroom. "I'll have my shower now. Get in bed."

"You said you were only bossy in the bedroom."

He stopped at the doorway to the bath and looked at her over his shoulder. "We are in the bedroom."

"Why don't you just admit you have oldest-child syndrome?"

His expression turned somber, though she didn't understand why. "Noted."

She would have teased that wasn't an admission, but Demyan disappeared into the bathroom.

Chanel didn't understand what was going on with him, but he wasn't leaving. She'd take that as a good sign.

Did he regret the implications toward the future he'd made before they had sex? Was he realizing now that he'd gotten his rocks off how ludicrous they'd been?

Maybe he thought she'd try to hold him to his words as if he'd made promises. She wouldn't.

Perhaps she needed to tell him that.

She crossed the room, but when she tried the door to the bath, it was locked.

She let her hand drop away. Okay, then.

Maybe she just needed to go to bed. Any talking could happen in the morning.

After only a few moments' deliberation, she opted to wear pajamas to bed. The mint-green jersey knit wasn't exactly sexy, but it was comfortable.

She was still awake when he joined her some indeterminate time later.

He didn't pause before pulling her into his

arms, though he made a sound of surprise when his hands encountered fabric. "Why are you wearing this?"

Because she'd needed a barrier between them, a level of armor, even if it was just her favorite pair of pj's. "Why not?" she answered rather than admit that, though.

"Because I prefer naked skin and I think you do, too."

"I wouldn't know. I've never slept with another person," she replied a tad acerbically.

"Perhaps it is for the best tonight. You will be too sore tomorrow if we make love again in the night."

"Oh." He still wanted her?

That was good, right?

"Do not sound so disappointed. We will make love again. Many times."

As promises for the future went, that was one she could live with. "I'm glad."

They were silent for several seconds before she offered, "Thank you for making my first time so special."

"I lost control." And there it was.

What was bothering him. She *knew* it.

"I liked it."

"I could have hurt you."

"But you didn't and I think it *would* have hurt me if you hadn't lost yourself just as badly as I did."

"Yes?" he asked, as if the concept was foreign to him.

"Absolutely."

"I am very glad to hear it." He'd turned out the light, but she could still hear the smile in his voice.

"Go to sleep."

"Your wish is my command."

She would have said something sarcastic about that blatant fabrication, but her mouth didn't want to work and she slipped into sleep, comforted by their banter.

Chanel was astonished by how easily she grew used to sleeping with someone else.

Not to the sex, though. She wasn't sure she'd ever grow *used to* the level of pleasure she and Demyan found in one another's bodies.

He *was* bossy in bed, just like he'd told her, but it was all targeted toward her enjoyment.

Every directive, every withholding of one instant gratification for something more was so that her final satisfaction was so incredibly overwhelming, she lost her mind with it.

But the sleeping together, that was different. That was all-night-long intimacy of another sort.

She, who had never even cuddled a bear in bed, found it difficult to sleep now when Demyan's arms weren't wrapped around her, his heartbeat a steady, comforting sound against her ear.

Hence her yawning this morning as she crunched the new data, despite three cups of coffee made in the new Keurig machine Demyan had gotten her.

He liked to buy her things, she'd noticed. Things *she* would like.

Her entire life, gifts had come with a subtle message to her to become something different. Designer clothes in a style unlike the one she favored, athletic shoes that were supposed to encourage her to take up running when she was perfectly happy with her tae kwon do training. Golfing gear, though she hated the game, a tennis racket despite the fact she'd never played.

But Demyan's pressies were different. They

were all targeted to the woman she was now, with no eye to making her into someone else. He showed an uncanny ability to tap in to her preferences, even when she'd never shared certain things with him.

Like her addiction to flavored coffees in direct opposition to her frustration over the complicated business of making a good cup of the beverage. So Demyan had found a way to feed the one while minimizing the other.

And the coffee? Delicious. And so darn easy.

She couldn't mess it up even when she got sidetracked by a new algorithm she wanted to try.

Even when she was sleepy from waking every couple of hours, reaching for him in the bed only to find empty space.

Demyan had left Seattle in the wee hours of the previous morning for what Chanel assumed was a business trip. She hadn't asked what it was about and he hadn't offered the information.

What she did know was that he wouldn't be back for two more days and an equal number of nights. Forty-eight more hours without him.

In the time line of life, it was hardly a blip.

So why did it feel longer than a particularly depraved man's purgatory to her?

Chanel already missed him with an ache that made absolutely no sense to her scientific brain. Okay, so they'd been dating a month now, not just three days. Making love and sleeping together every single night of the past three weeks of that month.

Still. How could she have become more addicted to his company than caffeine?

Because Chanel knew without any doubts she could go without coffee a heck of a lot more easily than she was finding it to be without her daily dose of Demyan.

She didn't know if she'd fallen in love at first sight like he'd hinted at three weeks ago, but she was in love with him now.

And that scared her more than a weekend at the spa with her mother.

"How close are you to closing the deal?" Fedir asked without preamble once he and Demyan were alone in the king's study.

Demyan's cousin and Gillian had returned from their honeymoon, and Queen Oxana wanted *family time.* That meant everyone in their small inner circle had come to the palace for a few days of "bonding."

Since his own parents would cheerfully go the rest of their lives without seeing Demyan, he never took Oxana's desire to spend time as a *family* for granted.

Though on this particular occasion, his mother and father and siblings were also staying at the palace in order to get to know their future queen, Gillian, better.

His father wouldn't make any effort to spend one-on-one time with Demyan, though. For all intents and purposes, Demyan's younger brother was his acknowledged oldest son.

Pushing aside old wounds Demyan no longer gave the power to hurt him, he answered his uncle's question. "She's emotionally engaged."

"When will you propose?"

"When I return."

Fedir nodded. "Smart. The time apart will leave her feeling vulnerable. She'll want to cement your bond. Women are like that."

Demyan didn't reply. His uncle was the last man, bar none, he would ask for advice on women.

"She'll sign the prenuptial agreement?"

"Yes." The more Demyan had gotten to know Chanel, the more apparent it had become that money was not a motivating factor for her.

She'd sign even the all-contingency prenuptial agreement Fedir's lawyers had drawn up simply because the financial terms would not matter to her.

"Good, good."

"I'll want changes made to some of the provisions before I present her with it, though."

Fedir frowned. "What? I thought the lawyers did a good job of covering all the bases."

"I want more generous monetary allowances for Chanel in the event our marriage ends in divorce or my death."

"What? Why?" Fedir's shock was almost comical. "Has a woman finally gotten under the skin of my untouchable nephew?"

Of course his uncle would immediately assume an emotional reason behind Demyan's actions. His sense of justice was a little warped by his all-consuming dedication to the welfare of Volyarus.

"I will do whatever I need to in order to protect this country, but I will do it with honor," Demyan replied.

"Of course, but your integrity is in no way compromised by your actions to insure the healthy future of our country."

Demyan wasn't sure he believed that. Regardless, he would minimize how much tarnish it took. "The terms will be changed to my requirements, or I won't offer the document to Chanel to sign."

As threats went, it wasn't very powerful. Baron Tanner's will had been clear and airtight. Chanel lost all claim to the baron's shares in Yurkovich Tanner upon marriage to any direct relation to the king.

"And without a prenup, there will be no wedding," Demyan added after several seconds of silence by his uncle.

"You don't mean that."

"When have you ever known me to bluff?" Demyan asked.

Fedir frowned. "She really does mean something to you."

"My integrity certainly does."

He was a ruthless man. Demyan knew that

about himself. He could make the hard choices, but he was an honest man, too. And he didn't make those choices without counting the cost.

"A man has to make sacrifices, even in that area for the greater good."

Demyan shrugged. "I'll contact the lawyers with the changes I want made to the agreement."

He wasn't going to debate his uncle's choices. The other man had to live with them and their consequences. It might be argued that everyone in the palace did, too, but Demyan wasn't a whiny child, moaning how his uncle's decisions had cost him his family.

The truth was, his own parents and their ambition were every bit as culpable.

"I'll trust you to be reasonable in your demands."

"I appreciate that."

"Demyan, you will never be king, but you are no less a son to me than Maksim." Fedir laid one hand on Demyan's shoulder and squeezed.

The words rocked through Demyan. His uncle was not an emotionally demonstrative man, in word or deed. Nor was he known for saying things he did not mean, at least not to family.

However, Demyan's cynicism in the face of life's lessons drove his speech. "A son you call nephew."

"A son I and all of Volyarus call prince."

"You never adopted me." According to Volyarussian law, which the king could change should he so desire, doing so would have made Demyan heir to the throne, not the spare.

He understood that, but it was also a fact that if he were truly every bit as much a son to Fedir, his place in the right of succession wouldn't have been a deterrent.

"Your parents refused."

Was Fedir trying to imply he'd asked? "I find that difficult to believe. They gave me up completely."

"But so long as you were legally their son, your father had leverage for his interests. He and your mother categorically refused to give that up."

His uncle's words rang true, particularly when weighed against how few of Demyan's father's efforts had met with support of the king since he'd become an adult. "I get my ruthlessness from him."

"But your honor is all your own. You are a better man than either of your fathers, the one by birth and the one by choice."

Fedir was not a man who gave empty compliments. So, Demyan couldn't help that the older man's words sparked emotion deep inside, but he wasn't about to admit that out loud.

"Oxana feels the same. She is very proud of both of her sons."

He thought of the excitement the queen had shown when Demyan had warned her that he'd found the one. "She wouldn't be proud of me if she knew why I'm pursuing Chanel."

"You're wrong. I am very proud of you." Oxana came into the room from the secret passageway entrance. "You have put the welfare of our people and your family ahead of your own happiness. How can I be anything but proud of that?"

Fedir started, clearly shocked his wife had been listening in.

"She's a special woman. She deserves a real marriage." It wasn't a sentiment Demyan would have expressed to Fedir without prompting, but this was Oxana.

She'd sacrificed her entire life for their country

and her family. Yet she was not a bitter woman. She loved them all deeply, if not overtly. She deserved to know that Demyan wasn't going to play Chanel for the sake of her inheritance.

"So, give her one." Oxana smiled with the same guarded approval she'd given him since he was a boy, though as he'd grown older he'd learned to look deeper for the true emotion. It was there. "She is a very lucky woman to have you."

Since he wasn't about to comment on the latter and the former was Demyan's plan, he merely nodded.

"That's not a reasonable request," Fedir said forcefully.

"For you, we all know that is true. But Demyan is a different man. A *better* man, by your own admission."

Fedir scowled at his wife of more than three decades. "He is our son. How can you demand he sacrifice the rest of his life for the sake of this girl's feelings?"

"How can you ask him to sacrifice his personal integrity to save our country?" Oxana countered, deigning to look at Fedir.

"He is not being dishonest."

"Oh, so you've told Chanel about her inheritance?" Oxana asked Demyan.

But he knew she wasn't talking to him, not really, so he didn't answer with so much as a shake of his head.

"How do you know about it?" Fedir asked Oxana, with shock lacing his usually forceful tones.

"It is in the historical archives for anyone to read."

"Anyone with access to the private files."

"I am queen. I get access."

Fedir opened his mouth and then shut it again without a word being uttered, his face settling into a frown.

Oxana turned to face Demyan, effectively cutting Fedir out of the conversation. "Promise me one thing."

"Yes." He didn't have to ask what it was. He trusted Oxana in a way he didn't trust anyone besides Maks.

If she wanted a promise, he would give it to her.

"Don't tell this woman, Chanel Tanner, that

you love her unless you mean it. Love isn't a bartering tool."

"She loves me." Chanel hadn't said so, but he was sure of it.

It's what he'd been working toward since he'd first walked into her office.

"No doubt. You are an eminently lovable man, but you owe it to her and to your own sense of honor not to lie about something so important."

"I never lied to you," Fedir inserted.

"Nothing has ever hurt as much as realizing Fedir had only said the words to convince me to give him the heir he needed for the throne."

"I did love you. I do love you."

Oxana spun to face her husband, but *not* her lover. "Like a sister. The few times you shared my bed, you called out *her* name at the critical moment."

This was so much more than Demyan wanted to know, but he saw no way of extricating himself from the situation. He could walk out easily enough, but he wouldn't leave Oxana to face the aftereffects of the emotional bloodletting that had been decades in the making.

"You knew about Bhodana from the beginning."

"You told me you loved me. I thought that meant you were going to let her go."

"I never promised you that."

"No, you were very careful not to."

"Oxana."

She waved her hand, dismissing him and his words as she turned back to Demyan. "You promise me, be the better man. Do not make declarations you don't mean."

"You have my word."

"I look forward to meeting her."

"I didn't plan to bring her here before the wedding."

"You don't want to scare her away."

"No." Unlike many women, Chanel was less likely to marry a prince than a normal man. "I've taken great care not to frighten her off."

"Does she know the real you?" Oxana asked.

He thought about their time in bed, intimacy during which his plans flew straight to heaven in the face of his body's response to Chanel. He'd try to convince himself that it would only be the first time, but subsequent sessions of lovemaking had proven otherwise.

"Yes," Demyan said. "She may not realize it, but definitely."

"Then all will be well. She is marrying the man you are at your core, Demyan, my son, not your title or the corporate shark who runs our company's operations so efficiently."

He hoped once Chanel saw his true persona and position, she would agree with her future mother-in-law. It was the one element to his plan that he could not be absolutely sure about.

With another woman, maybe, but with Chanel...learning he was a de facto prince could turn her right off him.

Excited anticipation buzzed through Chanel as the limousine taking her to meet Demyan rolled through the wet streets of Seattle.

His flight had arrived that morning, but he'd had a full day of meetings. Thankfully he'd told her about them before she offered to take a vacation day to spend with him.

Needy much?

She cringed at how much she'd missed him

and was fairly certain allowing him to see the extent of it might not be the best thing to do. Even someone as socially inept as Chanel realized that.

Still, it had been hard to play it cool and agree to let him send a driver for her without gushing over the idea of seeing him tonight and not having to wait until tomorrow.

They were attending an avant-garde live theater production downtown. No dinner. Demyan's schedule had not permitted.

Chanel was just glad he hadn't put off seeing her, but he'd seemed almost as eager to be with her as she felt about seeing him again. Considering the number of times their short phone call had been interrupted, she knew he'd had to force a slot into his schedule for her.

Knowing she was going to see him had made focusing on her work nearly impossible. Chanel had ended up taking the afternoon off and calling her sister for a last-minute shopping trip. Laura had helped Chanel pick out an outfit that was guaranteed to *drive the guy crazy.*

The sapphire-blue three-quarter-length-sleeve top was deceptively simple. With a scoop neckline outlined by a double line of black stitching and mock tuxedo tucking in the front, it was tailored in along her torso to emphasize her curves. The semi-transparent silk was worn over a bra in the same color. Not overtly slutty with the pleats in front, it still did a lovely job of highlighting Chanel's femininity.

The black silk trousers appeared conservative enough. Until she sat down, bent over or walked. Then the slit from midthigh to ankle hidden by the tuxedo stripe when she was standing gave intriguing glimpses of naked skin.

She'd never worn anything so revealing, but Laura insisted the peek-a-boo slit was interesting and not cheap. At the prices Chanel had paid for each piece of the outfit, she supposed *cheap* would not be a term that would ever apply to the clothing.

It had looked sophisticated in the boutique's full-length mirror, a little more scandalous in her own.

Laura had insisted on styling Chanel's ensemble as well, adding a demure rope of pearls knotted right below her breasts in an interesting juxtaposition that drew attention to the curves as effectively as the blue silk.

Her heels were strappy black sandals with what Laura called a *do-me-baby* heel. Chanel hadn't bothered to admonish her sister about the description.

She'd decided years ago that Laura was light-years ahead of Chanel in the girl-boy department. She didn't know if her baby sister was still a virgin like Chanel had been when she met Demyan, and honestly she had absolutely no desire to know.

The limousine slid to a halt and Chanel took a calming breath that did exactly no good.

She resisted the urge to pull at the carefully styled curls her sister had worked so hard to effect and waited for the driver to open the door.

It wasn't the chauffeur's hand reaching in to help her out of the limousine, though.

It was Demyan's, and his dark eyes glittered with lust as he took in her exposed thigh before meeting her gaze. "Hello, *sérdeńko*. I am very happy to see you."

She made no effort to stifle the smile that took over her features as she surged forward to exit the limo. If he hadn't been there with a steadying hand and then his arm around her waist, she would have fallen flat on her face.

But he *was* there and part of her heart was beginning to believe maybe he always would be.

He tucked her into his body protectively before leaning down to kiss her hello, right there in front of the crowd making their way into the theater.

She responded with more enthusiasm than probably was warranted, but he didn't seem to mind.

The kiss ended and he smiled down at her. "You look beautiful tonight. Very sexy."

"Laura played stylist."

"Your younger sister?"

"Yes. She's got even more acute fashion sense than Mom."

"Tell her I approve."

"She said you would."

His gaze skimmed her body. "Though I am not sure how I feel about everyone else seeing your body."

"They're just legs."

"Nice ones."

"It's the tae kwon do." Chanel's mother had heard somewhere that taking martial arts could improve Chanel's grace.

It hadn't done much for her poise and composure, but Chanel had discovered she *enjoyed* the classes. She'd insisted on continuing when her mother would have preferred she take a dance class.

Just one of many arguments between her and Beatrice during Chanel's formative years marked with parent-child acrimony.

"Then I am very grateful for your interest in Korean martial arts."

"You've never asked what color belt I am," she observed as he led her into the theater.

His thumb brushed up and down against her waist as if he couldn't help touching her. "What color?"

"Third-level black belt."

"Sixth-level black in judo," he said by way of reply.

"Want to spar?" she teased breathlessly.

The silk of her shirt transmitted the heat from his skin to hers and she wondered if she was the one who was going to end up teased to distraction by her outfit tonight.

"I spar with my cousin. I prefer less competitive physical pursuits with you."

She looked up into the side of his face, loving the line of his jaw, the way he held himself with such confidence. "Me, too."

He groaned.

"What?"

He stopped in the lobby and pulled her around so their gazes locked.

His was heated. "How can you ask what? You are dressed in a way guaranteed to keep my thoughts off the play and on what I plan to do to you once we get back to my condo."

CHAPTER SIX

HE SHOOK HIS HEAD as if trying to clear it. "What do you think has me groaning? It has been three nights."

She tried not to look as pleased as she felt, but was afraid she wasn't doing a very good job.

So she averted her head and met the envious gaze of another woman. Chanel ignored it, the envy having no power to pierce the bubble of happiness around her.

Demyan was with her and showed zero interest in being with, or even looking at, another woman.

She looked up at the sound of his laughter. He was watching her.

"I'm funny?" she asked.

"You are very pleased with yourself."

"I am happy with life, and you most of all," she offered.

She wasn't one to share her feelings easily, but

Laura hadn't spent the afternoon just coaching Chanel on fashion choices. Her little sister had told Chanel that if she really liked this man, she needed to open up to him.

"You can't do that thing you do with Mom and Dad and everyone else besides me and Andrew," Laura had said.

Even though Chanel thought she knew, she'd asked, "What thing?"

"The way you hold the real you back so no one can hurt her."

"You're pretty insightful."

"For a teenager, you mean."

"For anyone." Their mother was nearly fifty and Beatrice had less understanding of her oldest daughter's nature.

Demyan's hand slid down her hip, his fingertips playing across her exposed flesh through the slit.

Chanel gasped and jerked away from the touch.

His look was predatory. "I don't like to be ignored."

"I wasn't ignoring you."

"You weren't thinking about me."

"How can you tell?"

"I know."

"You're arrogant."

"So you have said, but you know I do not agree."

And the more she knew of him, the less she believed the accusation herself. There was a very hard-to-detect strain of vulnerability running through the man at her side. You had to look very closely to see it, but she watched him with every bit of her formidable scientist's brain focused entirely on one thing. Deciphering the data that made up Demyan Zaretsky.

"I'm thinking about you now," she promised.

"I know."

She laughed, feeling a light airiness that buoyed her through the crowd.

"Demyan!" a feminine voice called.

There was no mistaking the way his body tensed at the sound, not with him so close to Chanel as they walked.

He was coiled tightly, even as he turned them toward the woman who had called his name, with one of those fake smiles Chanel hadn't seen since their very first dates on his face. "Madeleine."

Madeleine's fashion sense and poise was everything Chanel's mother wished for her daughter.

Unfortunately, Chanel refused to make it a mission in life to live up to such hopes. She'd learned too young that nothing she did would ever be enough; therefore, what would be the point in trying to be someone she was not?

Madeleine's blond hair probably wasn't natural, but there were no telltale indicators. She wore her Givenchy dress with supreme confidence, her accessories in perfect proportion to the designer ensemble.

Chanel couldn't tell the other woman's age by looking at her but guessed it was somewhere between thirty and a well-preserved forty-five.

The look she gave Demyan said *he* knew her age, intimately.

If this had happened a month ago, Chanel would have withdrawn into herself and given up the playing field.

But what she'd denied on their third date was a certainty now. She was head over heels in love with Demyan Zaretsky, though she hadn't had a chance to tell him yet. Wasn't sure exactly when she wanted to.

While he'd never said the words, either, he hinted at a future together almost every time she saw him.

That love and his commitment to their future gave her strength.

Drawing on a bit of her mother's aplomb, Chanel stepped forward and extended her hand. "Chanel Tanner. Are you an *old* friend of Demyan's?"

Madeleine didn't miss Chanel's slight emphasis on the word *old,* her eyes narrowing just slightly with anger but no righteous indignation. So, she was older than she looked.

"You could say that." Madeleine put her hand on Demyan's sleeve. "We know each other quite well, though I admit I *didn't* know he wore glasses."

Demyan adroitly stepped away from the touch while keeping a proprietary arm around Chanel. "Is your husband here tonight, Madeleine?"

Stress made Chanel's body rigid. Had Demyan and this woman had an affair? He'd said he didn't believe in infidelity.

Had he been lying?

"He couldn't get away from the Microsoft people. I'm quite on my own tonight." Madeleine
smiled up at Demyan, her expression expectant.

It was clear she was angling for an invitation
to join them, though Chanel wasn't sure how
that was supposed to happen.

Their tickets had assigned seats.

Demyan ignored the hint completely. "The
cost of being married to a man with his responsibilities."

The older woman frowned again, this time
genuine anger lying right below the surface.
"Does your little friend here know that? Or is
she still in the honeymoon phase of believing
you'll make her a priority in your life?"

"She is a priority." He pulled Chanel closer.

She didn't know if the move was a conscious
one, but Madeleine noticed it, too.

That made Madeleine flinch and Chanel felt
unexpected compassion well up inside her. "I'm
sure you're a priority to your husband. He works
to make a good life for you both."

That's what she remembered her father saying to her mother.

"I knew what I was getting when I married him." Madeleine gave a significant look to Demyan. "And what I was giving up. I liked my chances with Franklin better."

"He married you. You read the situation right." There was a message in Demyan's voice for the other woman.

He was telling her *he* wouldn't have married her, and her words had put Chanel's mind at rest about the affair. Oh, it was clear the two had shared a bed at one time, but it was equally obvious that circumstance had ended before Madeleine married Franklin.

"How long were you two together?" Chanel asked with her infamous lack of tact but no desire to pull the question back once it was uttered.

It might be awkward, but it struck her how very little she really knew about Demyan.

"Didn't he tell you about me?" Madeleine asked, her tone just this side of snide.

And still Chanel couldn't feel anything but pity for her. She didn't look happy with her choices in life.

"No."

The other woman didn't seem happy with the

answer. Maybe Madeleine had thought she'd made a bigger impact on Demyan's life than she had. "You're a blunt one, aren't you? Did your mother teach you no tact?"

"To her eternal disappointment, no."

That brought an unexpected but small smile to Madeleine's lips.

Demyan leaned down and kissed Chanel's temple, no annoyance with her in his manner at all. "She is refreshingly direct," he said to Madeleine while looking at Chanel. "There is no artifice in her."

"So, she does not see the artifice in you," Madeleine opined, sounding sad rather than bitter.

"He holds things back," Chanel answered before Demyan could, but she did the older woman the courtesy of meeting her gaze to do so. "But if I know that, he's not hiding anything. I understand how hard it can be to share your true self with someone else."

"Heavens, don't you have *any* filters?" Madeleine demanded.

"No."

It was Demyan's turn to laugh, the sound genuine and apparently shocking to the other woman. Madeleine stared at him for a count of five full seconds, her mouth agape, her eyes widened comically.

Finally, she said, "I've never heard you make that sound."

"He's just laughing." Okay, so he didn't do it often, but the man had an undeniable sense of humor.

"*Just,* she says. This young thing really doesn't know you at all, does she?" Madeleine was the one looking with pity on Chanel now.

"It was a pleasure to run into you, but we need to find our seats. If you will excuse us," Demyan said, his tone brooking no obstacles and implying the exact opposite to his words.

Madeleine said nothing as they walked away.

When they reached their seats Chanel understood how the other woman had thought she might be included in their evening. Demyan had a box.

Although there was room for at least eight seats in it, there were only two burgundy-velvet-covered Queen Anne-style chairs. A small table with a bottle of champagne and two-person hors d'oeuvres tray stood between them.

Demyan led her to one of the seats, making sure she was comfortable before taking his own.

He looked out over the auditorium, stretching his long legs in front of him. "She's wrong, you know."

"Madeleine?"

"Yes."

"About what?"

He turned his head, looking at her in that way only he had ever done. As if she was a woman worthy of intense desire, of inciting his lust. "You know the man at the base of my nature."

"I hardly know anything about you." The words came from the scientist's nature even as her heart knew he spoke the truth.

That man who lost his control when he tried so hard not to, that man was the real Demyan.

Demyan shook his head, his dark eyes glowing with sensual lights she now recognized very well. "You know the most personal things about me."

"So does she."

"No."

"You had sex with her." And even though she now knew that Madeleine hadn't been married at the time, Chanel realized it still bothered her a little.

She knew he'd been with other lovers. Probably lots of them, but she really didn't want to keep running into them.

"She never saw the more primal side of my nature. No other woman has seen it."

"You think I know you better than anyone else because you don't show absolute control in the bedroom?" It's what she'd thought only seconds before, but saying it aloud made the very concept seem unreal.

"Yes."

"I want to know about your past. Not names of every woman you've been with. I hope I never meet another one, but I don't know *anything* about you." Except that to him, she was special.

She kept that to herself. She wanted more.

"It's the future that counts between us."

"But without a connection to the past, there is no basis for understanding the future." Historians made that claim all the time and scientists knew it to be true as well, for different reasons.

"I thought scientists were all about progress."

"Building on the discoveries of the past."

"Not making something entirely new?"

"Nothing is new, just newly discovered."

"Like your sexy fashion sense?" he teased.

"That's all Laura."

"I don't see Laura here now."

"I'd like you to meet her." If they had a future, they had to share their present lives.

Even the less-than-pleasant bits, which meant he'd have to meet her mother and Perry, as well.

"I would enjoy that very much."

"You would?"

"Naturally. She is your sister."

"A part of my past."

"And your present and your future."

"Yes, so?" she prompted.

He gave her a wary look she didn't understand. "You want to meet my family?"

"Very much. Unless... Do you not get on?" Maybe his relationship with his parents was worse than hers with Beatrice and Perry.

"I get on very well with the aunt and uncle who raised me."

"What happened to your parents?"

"Ambition."

"I don't understand."

"They gave me to be raised by my aunt and uncle to feed their own ambition."

There had to be more to the story than that, but she understood this was something Demyan didn't share with everyone. "Do you ever see them?"

"My aunt and uncle? Often. In fact, that's where I spent the last three days."

"I thought it was business."

"I did not say that."

"You didn't say anything at all."

"You did not ask."

"Do I have the right to ask?"

"Absolutely."

That was definitive and welcome. "Okay."

"My parents come to family social occasions," he offered without making her ask again, proving he'd known what she meant the first time around.

"And?"

"They do not consider me their son."

"Or their beloved nephew."

"Not beloved anything." His expression relayed none of the hurt that must cause him.

"I am sorry."

"You don't have it much better with your mother and Perry."

"I'm not sure I have it better at all," she admitted.

"Your parents do not understand you."

"They don't approve of me. That's worse, believe me." It would have been so much easier for her if her mother and Perry simply found her an enigma.

Instead, they considered her a defective model that needed constant attempts at fixing.

"I approve of you completely."

"Thank you." She grinned at him, letting her love shine in her eyes. She had a feeling the words weren't far from her lips, either. "I approve of you, too."

"I am very glad to hear that." He picked up the champagne bottle and poured them each a glass.

"Why champagne?" she asked.

If it was his favored wine of choice, she wouldn't ask, but he'd shared with her he drank champagne on only very special occasions.

He handed her a glass. "I'm hoping to have something to celebrate in very short order."

Goose bumps broke out over Chanel's skin, her heart going into her throat. "Oh?"

He reached into his pocket and brandished a small box that was unmistakable in size and intent.

"Isn't this supposed to happen after a five-course dinner and roses, and…" Her breath ran out and so did Chanel's words.

"I am not a man who follows other people's dictated scripts."

She had no trouble believing that. "Just your own."

Something passed through his eyes, almost like guilt, but that didn't make any sense. He might be bossy outside the bedroom a bit, too, but it was nothing to feel guilty about.

Chanel was no shrinking violet that she couldn't stand up to him if need be.

He moved, and suddenly he was on one knee in front of her, the ring box open and in his palm. "Marry me, Chanel."

"You… I… This… How can you want… It's only been a month…"

"Is longer than three dates. I knew I wanted

to marry you from the beginning." There could be no questioning the truth of that statement.

It was there in his eyes and voice. Nothing but honesty. He'd known he wanted her, had never wavered in that belief.

"What about love?"

"Do you love me?" he countered.

She nodded.

"Say it."

She glared. "You first."

"I may never say the words. You will have to accept that."

"If I want to marry you."

"Oh, you want to."

She did, but she didn't understand. "Why can't you say the words?"

"I can promise you fidelity and as good a life together as it is within my power to make for us. Is that not enough?"

The syntax change was odd and then she realized that as a native Ukrainian speaker, he was using the sentence structure of his first language. Did that mean he was nervous despite how calm and assured he appeared?

She looked at him closely and saw it, that small

strain of vulnerability she knew he'd rather she never witnessed. "I do love you."

"And I will always honor that."

"I don't know."

He flinched, uncertainty showing in his expression for a brief moment before his face closed. "You need time to consider it. I understand."

He stood up, pocketing the ring. "Lights will be going down momentarily for the play."

The gulf between them was huge, but she didn't know what to do to bridge it. She couldn't say *yes* right then. She didn't know if it was enough to never hear the words. Did not saying them mean he didn't feel the sentiment?

Maybe if he'd tell her *why* he couldn't say them, but clearly he didn't want to.

Still. He wanted to marry her. "Tell me why."

"Why, what?"

Was he playing dense, or did he really not know? "Why you won't say the words."

"I made a promise."

"To who?"

"The mother of my heart."

Chanel tried to understand. "She doesn't want you to get married?"

"Of course she does. She's very eager to meet you."

"But she doesn't want you to love me?" That didn't sound promising.

"She does not want me to use the words to convince you to marry me. It must be your decision entirely."

"Is this a Ukrainian thing?"

"We are not Ukrainian. We are Volyarussian."

Unlike their Ukrainian brothers, the Volyarussians had not been subject to Russian rule and loss of identity. Their ties to the old ways of doing and thinking from their original homeland were probably stronger than in the current Ukraine, but she understood what he was saying.

"Okay, a Volyarussian thing."

"It is a Yurkovich family thing."

"Your last name is Zaretsky."

"My parents never gave up legal rights."

"You could change your name now." He was an adult. There was nothing stopping him.

He jolted as if the idea had never occurred to him. Then he smiled. "Yes, I could."

"Maybe you should."

"Maybe if you agree to share it, I will change my last name to the one of my heart."

Those words played through Chanel's mind as the lights dimmed and the play began. She couldn't follow what was happening on the stage; she was too busy trying to figure out what was going on in Demyan's mind.

He'd asked her to marry him. He'd as good as told her he planned to, but she hadn't let herself believe.

She cast one of many glances in his direction, but his attention seemed riveted by the performance. He'd backed off so quickly, given up so easily.

That wasn't in character for him. Her certainty on that matter pulled her thoughts short. She'd claimed not to know him. He'd said she knew the man he was at his most basic nature. And she'd taken that to mean sexually.

But the truth was she knew him well in a lot of areas. He was a man driven by his own agenda, even ruthless in achieving it. The way he brought her pleasure, withholding both hers and his own until they'd reached *the* place indicated as much.

Demyan didn't give up easily, either. He pushed for what he wanted. Like convincing her to try making love while her hands were tied with silk scarves. She'd been leery and unwilling to do it, but he'd convinced her.

And it had been amazing.

Which begged the question: Did he not want her badly enough to fight, or was he sitting in that chair right now plotting how to get her while pretending to watch the actors on the stage?

She was pretty sure she knew the answer and it wasn't a disheartening one, though it was kind of alarming.

He was plotting, but she *wasn't* ready to give him an answer. Which meant she had to orchestrate a preemptive strike to prevent whatever it was he was planning. Probably to make love to her until she was an amenable pile of happy goo who would say *yes* to anything.

Not letting herself think about it too long and lose her nerve, Chanel scooted off her chair and onto the floor. Demyan's head snapped sideways so he could see her, proving he was highly attuned to what she was doing.

Definitely plotting.

"What are you doing?" he whisper-demanded.

She knee-walked the couple of feet between her chair and his. "You know, you could have opted for a more romantic setting. This would be easier if you'd had a settee brought in."

He stared at her, shock showing with flattering lack of artifice on every line of his handsome face. "What?"

"This." She reached for his belt.

He grabbed her wrist. "What are you doing?"

"You're repeating yourself and I would have thought it was obvious."

"Here?" he demanded, not sounding like himself at all.

She liked that. Very much.

In answer, she tugged her wrist free so she could undo the buckle on his belt. Once it was apart, she unbuttoned the waistband and then slowly and, as quietly as she could, she began to lower the zipper on his trousers in the darkened theater box.

No one could see her, though there were literally hundreds of people mere feet away.

The backs of her fingers brushed over an al-

ready erect shaft and a small laugh huffed out
of her.

"What is funny?"

"I was wrong."

"About?"

"I thought you were over here plotting, but the
truth is, you were thinking about sex, weren't
you?"

"Yes."

"Or were they one and the same?" she asked,
realizing belatedly the one did not necessarily
preclude the other.

He didn't answer, which was answer enough.

"We've done a lot of things."

His head nodded in a jerky motion.

"But not this."

"No."

"Why?"

"I did not know if you wanted to."

"You decided I wanted a lot of other things I
wasn't sure about."

"This is different."

Maybe it was. Maybe this had to come at her
instigation. "This is me, instigating."

"I do not understand."

She smiled at the confusion in his tone. "Here I thought you could read my mind."

"Not even I can do that."

Not *even* him. She almost laughed. "But you're not arrogant."

CHAPTER SEVEN

"CONFIDENT. NOT THE SAME." His words came out gritty and chopped, not at all like him.

Understandable and welcome in the circumstances.

"No, maybe it's not." She worked his hot shaft out through the slit in his boxers, thankful they were made from stretchy fabric. "I've never done this before."

"Do whatever you want. I promise to enjoy it."

She smiled. She believed him. There was one area of their relationship she was absolutely certain about and that was the amount of pleasure he took from their physical intimacy.

The man could not get enough of her.

So she didn't let herself worry if she was doing it right when she bent forward and licked around the head of his erection. It was wide and she knew she'd have to stretch her lips to get him inside. No way was much of him going to fit into her mouth, though.

She didn't worry about that right now, but concentrated on enjoying the taste of him. It was salty and kind of bitter, but sort of sweet, too. His skin was warm and clean and hot against her lips and tongue.

She liked it. A lot.

He didn't try to rush her, though a steady stream of pre-ejaculate was now weeping from his slit and his thighs were rock-rigid with tension. She jacked the bulk of his shaft with her hands while sucking on the end.

He made small, nearly nonexistent noises, letting her know he was enjoying this as much, or more, than she was.

Suddenly he grabbed her head and pulled it back, messing up the curls Laura had taken such effort to tame. "You have to stop."

"No."

"I'm going to come," he said fiercely.

"That's the point," she whispered back.

He shook his head. "You're not swallowing your first time. You don't know if you'll like it."

"You're being bossy again and this is not the bedroom."

Ignoring her less-than-stern admonition, he pulled her into his lap, maneuvering her so she could continue to touch him. Then he handed her a napkin from the table.

She grinned and almost asked what it was for to tease him, but the light in his eyes had gone feral. And really, she wasn't looking to get arrested for public indecency, which might well happen if his control slipped his leash completely.

So she finished him with her hand, catching his ejaculate with the napkin and his shout with a passionate kiss.

When he was done, he slumped in the chair, though his hold on her remained tight. "You did that on purpose."

"To give you pleasure?"

"That, too."

She snuggled into him. "I'm not giving you an answer tonight."

"Okay."

"Really?" She kissed under his chin, a little

startled by the reality of his suit and tie still pris-
tinely in place.

"Yes, but that will not stop me taking you back
to my condo and showing you what our married
life will be like."

"I've got no doubts about the great sex."

"We will make sure of that by morning."

"Should I call in at work tomorrow?" She
didn't want to try to do the complicated calcu-
lations for their current phase on no sleep.

And the look in his dark eyes said while she
might get to know his bed very well, she wasn't
going to be doing a lot of resting there.

"I think perhaps you should."

She did. In the early hours of the morning after
he made love to her through the night in his
condo that turned out to be a penthouse taking
up the entire top floor of one of the more his-
toric Seattle buildings.

Demyan woke her with kisses and caresses a
few hours later.

Their lovemaking was slow and almost tortur-
ous in its intensity. He seemed set on proving
something to her, but Chanel wasn't convinced

it was what she needed to know to agree to marry him.

When she was once again sated and relaxed, he informed her he'd called her sister and arranged to invite Chanel's entire family, including Andrew, whom he was flying up for the weekend in his private jet, for dinner the following evening.

"My parents are coming here?" Postcoital bliss evaporated like water pooled on a rock in the desert as she jumped out of his king-size bed and started pacing the darkly masculine bedroom. *"Tomorrow?"*

"Yes."

"Didn't you think you should ask me first?" she demanded.

Looking smug and certain of his answer, he said, "You were asleep."

"You could have waited until I woke up."

"I was bored."

"Right. And you had nothing else to occupy your time but calling my sister. How did you even get her number?" Had he gone snooping through her phone?

He averted his gaze without answering.

She sighed. "You got sneaky and underhanded, didn't you?"

It wasn't exactly a challenging conclusion to draw. As if there was any other way to get her sister's private cell number without waking and asking Chanel.

"The prospect does not make you angry?" he asked with a cautious look.

Nonplussed, she stared at him. "You aren't worried about how annoyed I am that you made plans with my family, just how irritated I am about your method for getting my sister's number?"

He shrugged.

"News flash—I find it a lot less upsetting that you scrolled through my phone's contacts while I was sleeping than the fact you used said contacts to set up a dinner with my family." She shook her head. "Well, this ought to be interesting."

With that, she went into the bathroom for a shower. It was her turn to lock the door.

Being the sneaky, underhanded guy he was, Demyan found his way inside regardless. Chanel hadn't expected anything else.

So she didn't jump when his hand landed on

her hip and his big body added to the heat behind her from the shower. "You told me you wanted me to meet your family."

"I said my sister," Chanel gritted out.

The man was far too intelligent not to have made the distinction.

He turned her in his arms, his expression more amused than concerned. "You know I will have to meet all of them eventually. Why not now?"

"Because I'm not ready!" She made no effort to control her volume, but she wasn't a yeller by nature, so the words came out sounding only about half as vehement as they did in her head.

The argument might have escalated, but he had the kissing-to-end-conflict technique down to a fine art.

They made love, moving together under the cascading water, his body behind hers, his arms wrapped around her so his hands could reach her most sensitive places.

As he brought her the ultimate in pleasure, he promised, "It will be all right, *sérdeńko*."

She desperately wanted to believe him, but a lifetime of experience had taught her otherwise. "You'll see me through their eyes."

"Or I will teach them to see you through mine."

Maybe, just maybe, his supreme self-confidence would guide his interactions with her family down that path.

She could hope.

The following night, her entire family showed up at Demyan's condo right on time.

Chanel was so happy to see Andrew and Laura that her stress at seeing her mother and stepfather didn't reach its usual critical levels instantly. That might also be attributed to the way Demyan kept one comforting arm around her throughout introductions and the launch into the usual small talk.

He'd brought in catering with servers so Chanel didn't have to cook or play hostess getting drinks. Somehow he'd known that those domestic social niceties had always been a source of criticism and failure with her family in the past.

She hadn't invited her parents to her apartment since moving out as a fresh-faced nineteen-year-old. Chanel had thought that having her own place would make a difference in how Beatrice and Perry responded to her efforts at cooking.

She'd learned differently quickly enough when they'd made it clear she fell short in every hosting department. The meal was too simple, the drinks offered too narrow in choice and even her bright stoneware dishes from a chain department store were considered inferior.

As could be inferred by her mother's gift of appropriate understated chinaware on Chanel's next birthday. She'd donated it to Goodwill and continued using her much less expensive, bright and cheerful dishes.

Since then, Chanel had assiduously avoided her mother's inferences and even direct suggestions that Chanel might like to host one of the smaller family get-togethers over the years. In the ten years since that first debacle, Chanel had made sure there were no situations in which she'd have to invite her mother or stepfather into her home for so much as a drink of water.

Perry was clearly impressed by Demyan as a host, though, the older man's expression shining with approval over the high-end penthouse and being offered his highball by a black-clad server.

Demyan kept them occupied with small talk, redirecting the conversation any time it looked like it would go into the familiar *let's-criticize-Chanel* direction. He was also overtly approving, verbalizing his appreciation for Chanel in ways that could not be mistaken or overlooked by her parents.

His protective behavior touched her deeply and Chanel found herself relaxing with her family in a way she could not remember doing in years.

"So, you work for Yurkovich Tanner?" Perry asked Demyan over dinner.

"I do."

Chanel added, "In the corporate offices."

A vague answer never satisfied her stepfather and she wasn't sure her addition would, either, but she could hope. She didn't want to spend the rest of the evening listening to Perry grill Demyan about his connections and job prospects.

She realized moments later that she needn't have worried.

Demyan adroitly evaded each sally until Perry gave up with a rather confused-sounding "Well, maybe you can put a good word in for Andrew. I tried contacting them on his behalf, you know, because of Andrew's connection to one of the original founders."

Andrew wasn't the one connected to Bartholomew Tanner. That was Chanel and her connection was tenuous at best, but trust Perry to dismiss her blood relationship to the founder and receipt of a Tanner Yurkovich university scholarship as unimportant altogether.

"I haven't heard back." Perry shrugged. "It was a long shot, but business is all about contacts."

Demyan nodded and then looked away from Perry to smile at Chanel. "I'm always happy to put a good word in for family."

Oh, the fiend. Chanel kicked Demyan's ankle under the table, but he didn't even have the courtesy to flinch.

So, that's why the dinner tonight. He'd said he was okay with waiting for her answer on his proposal, but really he had every intention of getting her family on his side. He had to realize it wouldn't take much.

Beatrice Saltzman had given up hope her oldest daughter would ever marry, and had never had any that it would be advantageously. She would be Demyan's biggest supporter once she realized the plans he wanted to make.

Chanel was going to kill him later, but right

now she had to deal with the fallout of his implication.

It wasn't her mother or Perry who picked up on it, either. They wouldn't

"You're getting married?" Laura gasped, her eyes shining. She grinned at Chanel. "I told you that outfit was going to hook him."

"I wasn't looking to *hook* anybody. We're not engaged."

"But I have asked Chanel to marry me."

Chanel's mother stared at her agape. "And you haven't said *yes?* No, of course you haven't." She shook her head like she couldn't expect anything else from her socially awkward eldest.

"I'm thinking about it." Chanel glared daggers at Demyan, but he smiled back with a shark's smile she was now convinced was *not* her imagination.

"Don't think too long. He's likely to withdraw the offer," Perry advised in serious, almost concerned tones. "You're not likely to do better."

"It's not a business deal." Chanel ground out the words, refusing to be hurt by her stepfather's observation.

Because it was true. She couldn't imagine anyone *better* than Demyan ever coming into her life, but that wasn't what was holding her back, was it?

"No, it's not," Andrew chimed in, giving his dad a fierce scowl. "Leave her alone about it. Demyan would be damn lucky to have Chanel for a wife and he's obviously smart enough to realize it."

Their mom tut-tutted about swearing, but Andrew ignored her and Chanel just gave her little brother a grateful smile. He and Laura had never taken after their parents' dim view of Chanel. Their extended family, other friends and colleagues of the Saltzmans might, but not her siblings.

For that, Chanel had always been extremely thankful. Because she loved Andrew and Laura to bits.

Instead of looking annoyed by Andrew taking Chanel's part, Demyan gave him an approving glance before turning a truly chilling one on Perry. "Neither of us is likely to do better, hence my proposal."

"Well, of course," Perry blustered, but no question—he realized he'd erred with his words.

Chanel wanted to agree to marry Demyan right then, but she couldn't. There was too much at stake.

Chanel was sitting down to watch an old-movie marathon on A&E when her doorbell rang the next evening.

She'd turned down Demyan's offer of dinner and a night in at the penthouse, telling him she wanted some time alone to think.

He hadn't been happy, insisting she could think as easily in his company as out of it. Knowing that for the fallacy it was, she'd refused to budge. No matter how many different arguments he brought to bear.

Chanel had taken the fact she'd gotten her way as proof she could withstand even the more forceful side of his personality. *And* that he respected her enough to accede to her wishes when he knew she was serious about them.

If he was the one ringing the bell, both suppositions would be faulty and that might be the answer she needed.

As painful as it might be to utter.

It wasn't Demyan through the peephole, though. It was Chanel's mom.

Stunned, Chanel opened the door. "Mother. What are you doing here?"

"I wanted to talk to you. May I come in?"

Chanel stepped back and watched with some bemusement as her mother entered her apartment for the first time since she'd moved in years ago.

Beatrice sat down on the sofa, carefully adjusting the skirt of her Vera Wang suit as she did so. "Close the door, Chanel. The temperature has dropped outside."

"Would you like something to drink?" Chanel asked as she obeyed her mother's directive and then hovered by the door, unsure what to do with herself.

"No, thank you." With a slight wave of her hand toward the other end of the sofa she indicated Chanel should sit down. "I… You seemed uncertain about your relationship with Demyan last night. I thought you might want to talk about it."

"To you?" Chanel asked with disbelief as she settled into her seat.

Her mother grimaced, but nodded. "Yes. I may not have been the best one these past years, but I am your mom."

"And he's rich." His penthouse showed that even to someone as oblivious as Chanel could be. Beatrice would have noticed and probably done a fair guesstimate of Demyan's yearly income off it.

"That's not why I'm here."

"He has corporate connections Perry and Andrew might find useful, too. I suppose that might carry even more weight with you." After all, scientists could be rich, but Beatrice had never made any bones about not wanting another one in the family.

Her mom sighed. "I am not here on behalf of your brother or my husband, either."

"You're here for my sake," Chanel supplied with full-on sarcasm.

But her mother nodded, her expression oddly vulnerable and sincere. "Yes, I am. The way you two are together. It's special, Chanel, and I don't want you to miss that."

"We've only been dating a month," Chanel

said, shocking herself and voicing her biggest concern.

Beatrice nodded, as if she understood completely. "That's the way it was for me and your dad. We knew the first time we met that we would be together for the rest of our lives."

"You stopped loving him." What would Chanel do if Demyan stopped wanting her?

Her mother's eyes blazed with more emotion than Chanel could ever remember seeing in them. "I never did."

"But you said…" Pain lanced through Chanel as her voice trailed off.

There were too many examples to pick only one.

"He was *it* for me."

"You married Perry."

"I needed someone after Jacob died."

"You had me. You promised we would always be a team." That broken promise had hurt worst of all.

"It was too hard. You were too much like him. I tried to make you different, but you refused to change." Her mother sighed, looking almost defeated. "You are so stubborn. Just like him."

For the first time, Chanel heard the pain in those words her mother had never expressed.

Some truths were just as hurtful to her. "Perry hates me."

"He's a very jealous man."

"He wasn't jealous of me. You weren't affectionate enough to me to make him jealous."

Sadness filled Beatrice's eyes. "No, I haven't been. He was jealous of Jacob."

"Because you never stopped loving him." Despite all evidence to the contrary.

"How do you stop loving the other half of your soul?"

Finally Chanel understood a part of her childhood she'd always been mystified by. She'd tried with Perry at first. Really tried. "Perry blamed me. He took his jealousy out on me."

"Your father wasn't around to punish."

"You let him."

Beatrice looked away and shrugged. As if it didn't matter. As if all that pain was okay to visit on a child.

"You let him," Chanel said again. "You knew and you let him hate me in effigy of my father."

Her mom's head snapped back around, her expression dismissive. "He doesn't hate you. He wanted you to be the best and all you wanted was your books and science."

"It's what I love. Didn't that ever matter to you?"

"Of course it mattered!" Beatrice jumped up, showing an unfamiliar agitation. "Science stole your father from me. Do you for one second believe I wanted it to take you, too?"

"So, you pushed me away instead."

"That wasn't my intention."

"I don't fit with the Saltzmans."

Beatrice didn't deny it, but she didn't agree either. Should Chanel be thankful for small mercies?

"I did fit with the Tanners."

"Too well, but they're all gone, Chanel. Can't you see that?"

"And you think I'll die young like Dad did because of my love for science?"

"You're too much a Tanner. You take risks."

"I don't!" She'd been impacted by the way her father and grandfather had died, too. "I'm very careful."

"If you are, then I've succeeded a little, anyway."

"You succeeded, all right. You succeeded in picking away at our relationship until there wasn't one anymore." Chanel nearly choked on the words, but she wouldn't hold them back anymore. "You couldn't handle how much having me around reminded you of Dad, so you pushed me away with both hands."

"And now you can barely bring yourself to see me even once a month."

"Visits with you are too demoralizing."

"Your sister and brother see you more often."

Even Andrew. He was away at university, but Chanel went to visit her brother at least once a term. She always made sure she got time with him when he was home. While she'd done her best to nurture her relationships with her siblings, Chanel had avoided her mother with the skill of a trained stunt driver.

"You have your sister date with Laura every week, but somehow you manage to avoid seeing me or Perry."

"Can you blame me?" Chanel demanded and then shook her head. "It doesn't matter if you do, or don't. I know whose fault it is we don't have a relationship and it's *not* mine."

Finally, she truly understood that. It wasn't that Chanel wasn't lovable. Unless she'd been willing to become a completely different person, with none of her father's passions, mannerisms or even affections, Chanel had been destined to be the brunt of both her mother's grief and Perry's jealousy.

There was no way she could be smart enough, well behaved enough or even pretty enough to earn their approval.

Not with hair the same color as her dad's and eyes so like his, too. Not with a jaw every Tanner seemed to be born with and her bone-deep desire to grow up and be a scientist.

Beatrice's eyes filled with grief that slowly morphed into resolution. "No, it's not. You deserved better than either Perry or I have given you. You deserve to be loved for yourself and by someone who isn't wishing every minute in your company you would move just a little differently, speak with less scientific jargon…"

"Just be someone other than who I am."

"Yes. You deserve that." Her mom's voice rang with a loving sincerity Chanel hadn't heard in it since she was eight years old and a broken vulnerability she *never* had. "That's why I'm urging you with everything in me not to push Demyan away because how you feel about him scares you. I wouldn't trade the years I had with your father for anything in the world, not even a life without the constant pain of grief that never leaves."

"You think Demyan loves me like Dad loved you?"

"He must." In a completely uncharacteristic gesture, Beatrice reached out and took both Chanel's hands in her own. "Sweetheart, a man like that, he doesn't offer you marriage when he could have you in his bed without it, not unless he wants all of you, but especially the life you can have together."

Her mother hadn't called her sweetheart in so long that Chanel had to take a couple of deep breaths to push back the emotion the endearment caused. "He's really possessive."

And bossy in bed, but she wasn't going to share that tidbit with her mom.

"He needs you. For a man to need that deeply, it's frightening for him. It makes him hold on tighter."

"Did Dad hold on tight?"

"Oh, yes."

Chanel had a hard time picturing it. "Like Perry?"

"Nothing like Perry. Jacob wasn't petty. Ever. He wasn't jealous. He trusted me and my love completely, but he held on tight. He wanted every minute with me he could get."

"He still followed his passion for science."

"Yes. I used to love him for it."

"You grew to hate him, though, didn't you?" That made so much sense.

Chanel hadn't just spent her childhood as scapegoat to Perry for a man who couldn't be reached in death. Her mom had punished her for being too like her father, too.

"I did." Tears welled and spilled over in Beatrice's eyes. "I betrayed our love by learning to hate him for leaving me."

Chanel didn't know what to do. Not only had she not seen her mother cry since the funeral, but they didn't have the kind of relationship that allowed her to offer comfort.

"He doesn't blame you." Chanel knew that

with every fiber of her being. Her dad's love for her mom had had no limits.

"For hating him? I'm sure you're right. He loved so purely. But if he were here now to see the damage I've done to you, to our bond as a family, he'd be furious. He *would* hate me, too."

CHAPTER EIGHT

CHANEL COULDN'T RESPOND.

Her throat was too tight with tears she didn't want to shed, but her mom was probably right.

Jacob Tanner had loved his daughter with the same deep, abiding emotion he'd given his wife. He'd expected a different kind of best from both of them than Perry ever had.

The good kind. The human kindness kind.

Beatrice sighed and swiped at the tears on her cheek, not even looking around for a tissue to do it properly. "I wish I could say I would do it all differently if I could."

"You can't?" Chanel asked, surprised at how much that hurt.

"As I have grown older and watched your brother and sister mature, had the opportunity to observe the way you are with them, it's opened my eyes to many things. I have come to realize just how weak a person I am."

"If you see a problem you have the power to fix and do nothing to change it, then yes, I think that does make you weak."

"So pragmatic. Your father would have said the same thing, but you both would have assumed I had the power to change myself. If I did, do you think I would have worked so hard at changing you?"

"So, that's it? Things go on like always?"

"No," Beatrice uttered with vehement urgency. "If you'll give me another chance, I will do better now."

"So, you *have* changed." Could Chanel believe her?

"I've acknowledged the true cost of my weakness. The love and respect of my daughter. It's too much."

"I don't know if I can ever trust you to love me."

"I understand that and I don't expect weekly mother-daughter dates."

"I don't have time." Chanel realized how harsh that sounded after she said the words, and she winced.

Her mom gave her a wry smile. "Your time

is spoken for, but maybe we could try for more often than once every couple of months."

"Let's see if we can make those visits more pleasant before we start making plans for more." Words were all well and good, but Chanel had two decades of her mother's criticisms and rejections echoing in her memories.

Beatrice nodded and then she did yet another out-of-character gesture, opening her arms for a hug. When Chanel didn't immediately move forward to accept, her mother took the initiative.

Chanel responded with their normal barely touching embrace, but her mom pulled her close in a cloud of her favorite Chanel No. 5 perfume and hugged her tight. "I love you, Chanel, and I'm very proud of the woman you've become. I'm so very, very sorry I wasn't a better mother."

Chanel sat in stunned silence for several seconds before returning the embrace.

"You don't think I'm too awkward and geeky for Demyan?" she asked against her mother's neck.

Still not ready to see the older woman's expression in case it wasn't kind.

But Beatrice moved back, forcing Chanel to

meet her eyes. "You listen to me, daughter. You are more than enough for that man. You are *all* that he needs. Now *you* need to believe that if you're going to be happy with him."

"It's only been a month, Mom."

"Your dad proposed on our third date."

The synergy of that took Chanel's breath away. Demyan hadn't proposed on their third date, but he'd told her then that they were starting something lifelong, not temporary. "I thought you got married because you were pregnant with me."

"I was pregnant, yes, but we'd already planned to get married. Only, our original plan was to do it after he finished his degree."

"You said…"

"A lot of stupid things."

Chanel's mouth dropped open in shock at her mother's blunt admission.

Beatrice gave a watery laugh. "Close your mouth. You'll catch flies."

"I love you, too, Mom."

"Thank you. That means more than you'll ever know. I know I don't deserve it."

"I didn't say I liked you," Chanel offered with her usual frankness and for once didn't regret it.

Their relationship was going to work only if they moved through the pain, not try to bury it.

"You will, sweetheart. You loved your daddy, but I was your favorite person the first eight years of your life."

"I don't remember." She didn't say it to belabor the point. She just didn't.

"You will. I'm stubborn, too. You didn't get it all from Jacob."

"What about Perry?"

"I'll talk to him. I guess I never realized how bad it was in your mind between you. He really doesn't hate you. He's even told me he admires you."

Chanel made a disbelieving sound.

"It's true. You're brilliant in your field. I think it intimidates him. He's a strong businessman, but if he had your brains he'd be in Demyan's position."

With a penthouse with a view of the harbor? Her parents lived in the suburbs and she couldn't imagine them wanting anything different.

Her mother left soon thereafter, once she'd promised again to change and make sure Perry knew he had to alter the way he interacted with Chanel, too.

No one could have been more shocked than Chanel when she got a call from the man himself later that night. He apologized and admitted he'd thought she had always compared him unfavorably to her dad, just like her mom did.

Chanel didn't try to make him feel better. Perry did compare unfavorably with Jacob Tanner. Her dad had been a much kinder and loving father, but Chanel agreed to try to let the past go if the future was different.

How had Demyan affected such change in her life in so little time? She wasn't going to kid herself and try to say it was anything else, either.

Somehow Demyan had blown into her life and set it on a different path, one in which she didn't have to be lonely or rejected anymore.

If she could let herself trust him and the love she felt for him, the rest of her life could and would be different, too.

She picked up the phone and called him.

"Missing me, little one?" he asked without a greeting.

"Yes." There was a wealth of meaning in that one word, if he wanted to hear it.

"*Yes* as in yes, you miss me, or *yes* as in you will marry me?" he asked, sounding hopeful but cautious.

"Both."

"I will be there in ten minutes."

It was a half-hour drive from his penthouse, but she didn't argue.

Demyan knocked on Chanel's door with a minute to spare in the ten he'd promised her.

What he hadn't told her when she called was that he was already in the area.

The door swung open, and Chanel's eyes widened with disbelief. "How did you get here so fast?"

"I was already on the road." Had been for the better part of an hour, driving aimlessly, with each random turn taking him closer and closer to her apartment complex.

She frowned. "On your way here?"

"Not consciously." He'd argued with himself about the wisdom of calling or stopping by after she'd told him she wanted the night to think.

So far, respecting her wishes had been winning his internal debate.

"Then what were you doing over here?"

He gently pushed past her, not interested in having this discussion, or any other, on the stoop outside her door. "I was out for a drive."

"On this side of town?" she asked skeptically.

"Yes."

"But you weren't planning to come by."

"No." And that choice had clearly been the right one, though more difficult to follow through on than he wanted to admit.

"Do you go out for drives with no purpose often?" she asked, still sounding disbelieving.

"Not as such, no." He went through to the kitchen, where he poured himself two fingers of Volyarussian vodka before drinking half of it in two swallows.

He'd brought the bottle with him one night, telling her that sometimes he enjoyed a shot to unwind. She'd told him he could keep it in the freezer if he liked.

He did, though he rarely drank from it.

"Are you okay, Demyan?" she asked from

the open archway between her living room and kitchen. "I thought you'd be happy."

"I didn't like the emptiness of my condo tonight." He should have found the lack of company peaceful.

A respite.

He hadn't. He'd become too accustomed to her presence in the evenings. Even when she only sat curled up with one of her never-ending scientific journals while he answered email, having her there was *pleasant.*

Had almost become necessary.

"I missed you, too."

"You wanted your space. To think," he reminded her, the planning side of his facile brain yelling at him that his reaction wasn't doing his agenda any favors.

"It was fruitful. Or have you forgotten what I told you on the phone?"

He slammed the drink onto the counter, clear liquid splashing over the sides, the smell of vodka wafting up. "I have not forgotten."

Her gray eyes flared at his action, but she didn't look worried. "And you're happy?"

"Ecstatic."

"You look it." The words were sarcastic, but an understanding light glowed in her lovely eyes.

"You are a *permanent fixture* in my life. It is only natural I would come to rely on your companionship to a certain extent." He tried to explain away his inability to remain in his empty apartment and work, as he'd planned to.

A small smile played around her mobile lips. "So, you considered me a permanent fixture before I agreed to marry you?"

"Yes." He was not in the habit of losing what he went after.

"I see. I wasn't nearly so confident, but I missed you like crazy when you were in Volyarus."

"And yet you refused my proposal at first."

"I didn't. I told you I had to think."

"That is not agreement."

"Life is not that black-and-white."

"Isn't it?"

"No." She moved right into his personal space. "I think you're even more freaked out by how fast everything has gone between us than I am."

"I am not." It had all been part of his plan, everything except this inexplicable reaction to her request for time away from him.

"You're acting freaked. Slamming back vodka and driving around like a teenager with his first car."

"I assure you, I did not peel rubber at any stop-lights."

"Do teens still do that?"

"Some." He never had.

It would have not been fitting for a prince.

"I said yes, Demyan." She laid her hands on his chest, her eyes soft with emotion.

His arms automatically went around her, locking her into his embrace. "Why?"

Her agreement should have been enough, but he needed to know.

"My mom came by to talk. She told me not to give up on something this powerful just because it scares me."

"Your mother?" he asked, finding that one hard to take in.

"Yes. She wants to try again, on our relationship."

"She does realize you are twenty-nine, not nineteen?"

Chanel smiled, sadness and hope both lurking in the storm-cloud depths of her eyes. "We both do. It's not happy families all of a sudden, but I'm willing to meet her partway."

"You're a more forgiving person than I am."

"I'm not so sure about that, but one thing I do know. Holding bitterness and anger inside hurts me more than anyone who has ever hurt me."

A cold wind blew across his soul. Demyan hoped she remembered that if she ever found out the truth about her great-great-grandfather's will.

She frowned up at him. "You were driving without your glasses?"

"I don't need them to drive." He didn't need them at all but wasn't sure when he was going to break that news to her.

"You always wear them, except in bed."

"They're not that corrective." Were in fact just clear plastic.

"They're a crutch for you," she said with that analytical look she got sometimes.

"You could say that."

"Do you need them at all?"

He didn't even consider lying in answer to the direct question. "No."

He expected anger, or at least the question, *why did he wear them?* But instead he got a measured glance that implied understanding, which confused him. "If I can step off the precipice and agree to marry you, you can stop wearing the glasses."

The tumblers clicked into place. She saw the glasses as the crutch she'd named them for him. Being who she was, it never occurred to her that they were more a prop.

"Fine." More than. Remembering them was a pain.

She grinned up at him and he found himself returning the expression with interest, a strange, tight but not unpleasant feeling in his chest.

"Want to celebrate getting engaged?" she asked with an exaggerated flutter of her eyelashes.

The urge to tease came out of nowhere, but he went with it. "You want a shot of my vodka?"

He liked the man he became in this woman's presence.

"I was thinking something more *mind-blowing* and less about imbibing and more about experiencing." She drew out the last word as she ran her fingertip across his lips, down his face and neck and on downward over his chest, until she stopped with it hovering right over his nipple.

He tugged her closer, his body reacting as it always did to her nearness. "I'm all about the experience."

"Are you?" she asked.

He sighed and admitted, "Not usually, no. My position consumes my life."

"Not anymore."

"No, not anymore." He hadn't planned it this way, but marrying Chanel Tanner was going to change everything.

He could feel it with the same sense of inevitability he'd had the first time he'd seen her picture in his uncle's study. Only now he knew marrying her wasn't going to be a temporary action to effect a permanent fix for his country.

And he was glad. The sex *was* mind-blowing, but that didn't shock him as much as it did her. What *he* hadn't anticipated was that her company would be just as satisfying to him, even when it came without the cataclysm of climax.

Right now, though? He planned to have both.

* * *

Chanel adjusted her seat belt, the physical restraint doing nothing to dispel the sense of unreality infusing her being.

Once she'd agreed to marry Demyan, he'd lost no time setting the date, a mere six weeks from the night of their engagement. He'd told her that his aunt wanted to plan the wedding.

Chanel, who was one of the few little girls in her class at school who had not spent her childhood dreaming of the perfect wedding, was eminently happy to have someone else liaise and plan with her mother. Beatrice was determined to turn the rushed wedding into a major social event.

And the less Chanel had to participate in that, the better. If she could have convinced Demyan to elope, she would have, but he had this weird idea that she *deserved* a real wedding.

Since she'd made it clear how very much she *didn't* want to be the center of attention in a big production like the type of wedding her mother would insist on, Chanel had drawn the conclusion the wedding was important to Demyan.

So, she gave in, both shocked and delighted to

learn that her mom had agreed to have the wedding take place in Volyarus with no argument.

Beatrice had been vague when Chanel had asked why, something about Demyan's family being large and it only being right to have the wedding in his homeland. Chanel hadn't expected that kind of understanding from her mom and had been glad for it.

She'd even expressed genuine gratitude to Beatrice for taking over the planning role with Demyan's aunt. Chanel had spent the past weeks working extra hours so she could leave her research in a good place to take a four-week honeymoon in Volyarus.

She hadn't been disappointed at all when Demyan had asked her if she'd be willing to get to know his homeland for their honeymoon.

She loved the idea of spending a month in his company learning all she could about the small island country and its people, not to mention seeing him surrounded by family and the ones who had known him his whole life.

There was still a part of Chanel that felt like Demyan was a stranger to her. Or rather a part of Demyan that she did not know.

Her mother had flown out to Volyarus two weeks before to finalize plans for the wedding with Demyan's aunt. Perry, Andrew and Laura were on the plane with Chanel and Demyan now.

Perry *had* made a determined effort not to criticize her, but Chanel couldn't tell if that was because of her mother's talk with him or out of deference for Demyan. She'd never seen her stepfather treat someone the way he did Demyan, almost like business royalty, or something.

It made Chanel wonder.

"What is it you do at Yurkovich Tanner?" she asked as the plane's engines warmed up.

Demyan turned to look at her, that possessive, content expression he'd worn since the morning after she agreed to marry him very much in evidence.

"Why do you ask?"

"Because I realized I don't know."

"I am the Head of Operations."

"In Seattle?" she asked, a little startled his job was such a high-level one, but then annoyed with herself for not realizing it had to be.

Only, wasn't it odd for the corporate big fish

to personally check out the recipients of their charitable donations?

"Worldwide," he said almost dismissively. "My office is in Seattle."

"I knew that, at least." Worldwide, as in he was Head of Operations over all of Yurkovich Tanner?

She'd done a little research into the company after they gifted her with a university education. It wasn't small by any stretch. They held interests on almost every continent of the world and the CEO was the heir apparent to the Volyarussian throne.

That Demyan was Head of Operations meant he swam with some really exalted fish in his tank.

"You are looking at me oddly," Demyan accused.

"I didn't realize."

He brushed back a bouncy curl that had fallen into her eye, his own expression intent. "Does my job title matter so much?"

"I know your favorite writer, the way you like your steak and how many children your ideal family would have, but I don't know anything about your job."

"On the contrary, you know a great deal. You

have sat beside me while I took conference calls with our operations in Africa and Asia."

"I tuned you out." Corporate speak wasn't nearly as interesting as science…or her erotic readings.

Now that she had practical experience, they were even more fascinating.

He smiled with a warm sincerity she loved, the expression almost common now. At least when directed at her. "You did not miss anything that would interest you."

"I figured." She sighed. "I just feel like I should understand this side of your life better. You work really long hours."

So did she, but it occurred to her that maybe his long hours weren't going to go away like hers now that she'd caught up on work for her extended honeymoon.

"It is a demanding job."

"Do you enjoy it?"

"Very much."

"Will you continue working twelve- to sixteen-hour days after we get back from Volyarus?"

"I will do my best to cut my hours back, but twelve-hour days are not uncommon."

"I see. Okay, then."

"Okay, what? You have that look you get."

"What look?"

"The stubborn one." His brows drew together. "The same one you got when you insisted on buying your wedding dress without your mother's or my aunt's input."

Demyan's aunt, Oxana, had offered a Givenchy gown. Chanel had turned her down. Demyan hadn't been happy, wanting to save Chanel the stress and expense of searching for the perfect dress. He knew clothes were not usually her thing, but Chanel refused to compromise on this issue.

While she couldn't really care less about the colors for the linens, what food would be served or even the order of events at the reception, there were two things Chanel did care about.

What she wore and who officiated.

On the officiate, she'd agreed to have Demyan's family Orthodox priest perform the service so long as the pastor from the church she'd attended since childhood, a man who had known and respected both her father and grandfather, led them in their personally written vows and spoke the final prayer.

Her dress she wasn't compromising on at all. Chanel and Laura had spent three weeks haunting eBay, vintage and resale shops, but they'd finally found the perfect one.

An original Chanel gown designed by Coco herself.

Because while her mother had named Chanel after her favorite designer, she'd also named her after the designer she'd been wearing when Chanel's dad proposed. Chanel had wanted a link to her dad on her wedding day and wearing the vintage dress was it.

The rayon lace overlay of magnolia blossoms draped to a demure fichu collar. However, the signature Coco Chanel angel sleeves with daring cutouts gave the dress an understated air of sexiness she liked.

The dress was designed to enhance a figure like Chanel's. Clinging to her breasts, waist and hips only to flare slightly from below the knee, the gown made her look and feel feminine without being flouncy and constrictively uncomfortable.

Buying it had nearly drained Chanel's savings account and she really didn't care. Her job paid well and Demyan wasn't exactly hurting for cash.

Demyan's mouth covered Chanel's and she was kissing him before she was even conscious he'd played his usual *get-Chanel's-attention-when-her-mind-is-wandering* card. She had to admit she liked it a lot more than the sharp rebukes she got from others because of her habit of getting lost in thought.

After several pleasurable seconds, he lifted his head.

Dazed, she smiled up at him even as she was aware of her brother making fake gagging gestures in his seat across the aisle.

Perry shushed him, but Chanel paid neither male any heed.

She was too focused on the look in Demyan's eyes. It was so warm.

"That's better," he said.

"Than?"

"You thinking about something else. You're only thinking about me, now."

She laughed softly. "Yes, I am."

CHAPTER NINE

"WHAT PUT THAT stubborn look on your face before?"

She had to think and then she remembered. "You said you worked twelve-hour days, usually."

"I did and you said that was okay."

"No, I said *okay* in acknowledgment."

"You do not approve of twelve-hour days."

She shrugged. "That's not really the issue."

"It's not?"

"No."

"What is the issue?"

"Children."

His brows drew together like he was confused about something. "We agreed we wanted at least two."

He'd figure it out. He was a smart man.

"We also agreed that because of health considerations and family history, I wouldn't get pregnant after thirty-five."

"So?"

"So, we may have to adjust for an only child, or no children at all."

"Why?" he asked, sounding dangerous, the expression on his gorgeous face equally forbidding.

"Children need both parents' attention."

"Not all children have two parents."

"But if they do, they deserve both of those parents to make them a priority."

"I will not shirk my responsibility to my children."

"A dad does more than live up to responsibilities. He takes his kids to the beach in sunny weather and attends their soccer games. You can't do that if you're working twelve-hour days five days a week."

Something ticked in his expression.

Her heart sank. "You work weekends."

"Thus far, yes."

Was this a deal breaker? No.

But she didn't like figuring it out now, either. "I'll volunteer with after-school programs," she decided. "I don't have to have children to have a complete life."

"You are threatening not to have children if I do not cut my hours?"

"I'm not threatening. I'm telling you I'm not bringing any children into this world who are going to spend their childhoods wondering how important they are to their dad, if at all."

"And you accuse me of seeing the world in only two colors."

"I see lots of shades and shadows. That doesn't mean my children are going to live under one or more of them."

"Have you never considered the art of compromise?"

"I suck at it." Hadn't he realized that already? She gave in on what didn't matter, and on what did? Well, she could be a bit intransigent.

"This may be a problem. I am not known for giving in on what matters to me." He said it like she might not know.

"It's a good thing we agree on this issue, then."

Demyan didn't look comforted. "How is that?"

"You said you wanted to be the best father possible, that you never wanted your children to doubt their place in your life."

"Yes."

"Then you agree it is better not to have them if your work schedule isn't going to change."

He looked tired suddenly, and frustrated. "It is not that simple."

"It can be."

"What do you suggest? That I let Yurkovich Tanner run into the ground?"

"I suggest you hire three assistants, one for each major market, men and women who know the company, who care about it and that you trust to make minor decisions. They're the first line for policy and decision making, leaving you open to spend your time on only the most high-level stuff."

"And if that's all I work on already?"

"It's not."

"You told me you tuned out my calls."

"That doesn't mean I can't access the memories."

"You're scary smart, aren't you?"

She shrugged, but they hadn't even bothered finishing her IQ test in high school after she completed the first three exercises before the tester even got the timer going. The teacher hadn't wanted her to feel like a freak.

If only he'd been able to coach her parents.

"You just found out what my job is and you're already giving advice on it." Far from annoyed, Demyan sounded admiring.

"I'm a quick thinker."

"You'd be brilliant in business."

"No interest." Much to both her mother's and Perry's distress.

"I'll talk it over with my uncle."

"Is he your business mentor?"

"He's my boss."

"He works for Yurkovich Tanner?"

"He's the King of Volyarus."

She waited for the rest of the joke, only it didn't come, and the look Demyan was giving her said it wasn't going to.

She knew that ultimately the ownership of Yurkovich Tanner resided with the monarchy of that country. However, the thought that Demyan's uncle and the king were one and the same person had never entered her mind.

"Your uncle is a king."

"Yes."

"Oxana?"

"Queen."

"She told me to call her Oxana."

"That is her privilege."

Chanel felt like she was going to be sick. "You never said."

"I didn't want to scare you off."

"Holding back important information is like lying."

"I'm called Prince Demyan, but I'm no knight in shining armor. At heart I am a Cossack, Chanel. You must realize that. Any armor I have is tarnished. I am a human man with human failings." He said it as if admitting a darkly held secret.

Another time, she would have teased him about his melodrama and the arrogance behind it. Right now? She needed to think.

"I wasn't expecting this. You're this corporate guy who wears sweaters." Only, he hadn't been wearing them, or the jeans, so much lately.

She hadn't really noticed, until now. Clothing didn't matter much to her. She wasn't her mother, or even Laura in that regard. But looking back, she realized there had been a lot of subtle changes over the past six weeks.

He dressed in suits so sharp they could have

come out of the knife drawer. She hardly ever saw the more casual attire he'd been wearing when they first met. Sometimes in the evenings, but he never left the house in the morning wearing a sweater.

She never noticed him reaching to adjust glasses that weren't there anymore, either.

Which meant what? That he was a lot more confident than she'd thought.

Okay, anyone who thought Demyan Zaretsky lacked confidence needed to take a reality check. Her included.

She didn't know why he'd worn the glasses, but they weren't a crutch for some deep-seated insecurity.

And honestly, did that matter right now?

"Chanel," he prompted.

She stared at him, trying to make the difference between *who* he was and *what* he was make sense through the shock of his revelation. "You're a prince."

"It's a nominal title only."

"What does that even mean?" What she knew about royalty wouldn't fill a page, much less a book.

"Officially, I am a duke, but I am called prince at the pleasure of my uncle, the king."

"The one who raised you?" Still not making sense, and getting cloudier rather than clearer.

"He and Oxana raised me as a brother to Maksim, the Crown Prince. I was spare to the throne."

"Was?"

"My cousin's wife is expecting their first child."

"Next in line to the throne now?"

"Yes."

"It's just all so strange."

She looked around the plane, which had taken off at some point but she couldn't have said when. Her family were all staring, making no effort to hide their interest.

Perry didn't look surprised at all, but Andrew's and Laura's eyes were both saucer wide.

"Mom and Perry knew," she guessed.

"Yes."

"They never said."

"They agreed my position might scare you off me. I wanted time to show you *I* am the man you promised to marry."

"But *you* are a prince."

"Does that change how you feel about me?" he demanded, no give for prevarication in his voice.

There were a lot of conflicting things going on inside Chanel, but this wasn't something she was in any question about. "No. I love you, not what you are."

"I am glad to hear it." The relief in his tone couldn't be faked.

"This is so cool," Andrew said, reminding Chanel of their audience.

She frowned at her little brother. "You might think so."

"I do, too," Laura said.

"The only thing that matters is what you think," Demyan said from beside her.

"The jury is still out on that one."

"Don't be flip."

She glared up at him. "I'm not. I mean it. Give me some time to process."

"Chanel—"

"No. I don't want to talk about it right now."

She didn't want to talk at all, and shut down every attempt either he or her family made on the rest of the flight, going so far as to feign

sleep to get them all to just leave her alone for
a bit.

Life had changed so fast and she'd thought
she'd come to terms with that, but Demyan was
still throwing her curveballs and Chanel had
never been good at sports.

Their arrival in Volyarus was less overwhelming
than she might have expected given Demyan's
position.

Thankfully, there was no fanfare, no line of
reporters with oversize cameras. Of course if
there had been, she would have shown them all
just how she'd gotten her black belt in tae kwon
do, with Demyan as her unwitting assistant in
the endeavor.

However, other than some official-looking
men who looked like they were straight off
the set of *Men in Black,* there were only two
other people—Chanel's mother and a beautiful woman with an unmistakable regal bearing.
Queen Oxana.

Demyan guided Chanel toward the two women
with his hand on the small of her back. He

stopped when they were facing his aunt and he introduced them all.

The queen put her hand out to Chanel. "It's a pleasure to meet you. Demyan speaks very highly of you, as does your mother."

Chanel did her best not to show her surprise.

She knew Beatrice was trying, but the idea she had actually *complimented* Chanel to the other woman was still too new to be anything but startling. Oxana had spent the past two weeks in Beatrice's company. In the past, Chanel would have been sure the results would be catastrophic for any hopes she might have of gaining the queen's regard.

From the look of both women, that wasn't something she had to worry about anymore.

Unexpected and warm pleasure poured through Chanel's heart, filling it to the brim, and she smiled at her mother before squeezing the queen's hand. "Thank you for making Demyan a part of *your* family. Someone taught him how to protect the people he cares about and I think that was you."

The lovely dark eyes widened, Oxana's mouth parting in shock and then curving into an open smile. "I believe he will be in very good hands with you, Chanel."

The king was waiting at the palace when they arrived, his manner more reserved and less welcoming to Chanel. She didn't mind.

She thought she understood.

Everyone else was acting as if it was perfectly normal for a prince to get engaged after a month and married six weeks later.

Obviously, King Fedir had his qualms about it.

Since Chanel still had her own fears, she had no problem with the fact he might have some, as well.

Wedding plans made it impossible for Chanel and Demyan to have any time alone for the rest of the day. She was not surprised to find him in her room late that night after she left her mother and the indefatigable Oxana still discussing seating charts.

Demyan pulled Chanel into his arms and kissed her for several long seconds before stepping back. "That is better."

"You missed me."

"I spend all day without you at work."

"But it was different here."

"Yes."

"Worried the mom of your heart would let slip too many of your secrets?" she teased, unprepared for the clearly guilty look that crossed his features. "What?"

He shook his gorgeous head. "Nothing."

"Demyan?"

"She is the mother of my heart."

"Have you told her and the king you filed for an official name change?"

"They will hear when the priest names me during the ceremony."

"You're a closet romantic, aren't you?"

"I am no romantic, Chanel."

"You just go on thinking that." Then a truly horrific thought assailed her. "Are people going to call me Princess after we are married?"

"Are you going to refuse to marry me if I say yes?" he asked, sounding way too serious.

"I'm not going to refuse to marry you, but Demyan, it's not easy, this finding-out-you're-royalty thing."

He nodded, as if he understood, but how could he? He'd grown up knowing what he was.

"So, about the princess thing…" She wasn't willing to let this go. Chanel wanted an answer.

He'd left enough out up to this point.

"That depends on my uncle."

"If he calls me princess…"

"Then others will."

"Oh." Considering the cool reception she'd received from King Fedir, she didn't think he was going to call her princess anytime soon.

"You look relieved."

"I'm not a princess in his eyes." As she said the words, she knew them to be absolute truth. And she didn't blame King Fedir for feeling that way. "I'm not nobility."

"You are. You inherited the title from your great-great-grandfather—you are a dame. Marrying me will make you a duchess."

"So?"

"So, even if you are not called princess, most will call you by your title." His expression and tone said he was perfectly aware she wasn't going to see that truth as a benefit to marriage.

"That's medieval."

"No. Trust me, the nobility system is alive and well in many modern countries."

"But…" She didn't want to be called duchess.

"The correct term is Your Grace."

"That makes me sound like, like… What do they call them, a cardinal or something in the Catholic church."

He laughed, like she'd been joking.

She wasn't. "I'm… This is…"

He didn't let her keep floundering. Showing he knew exactly what Chanel needed—him—Demyan pulled her into his arms and kissed her.

All thoughts of unwanted titles and unexpected ties to royalty went flying from her head in favor of one consuming emotion. Love for the man so intent on making her his wife.

Over the next few days, Chanel hardly saw Demyan—except when he came to her room at night and made passionate, almost desperate love to her.

She didn't understand, but it felt like he was avoiding her. Not sure that wasn't her old insecurities talking, she refused to voice her concerns aloud.

He didn't seem inclined to anything serious for pillow talk either, but she understood that.

Chanel certainly didn't want to talk about the wedding and its never-ending preparations and plans. Nor was she interested in discussing her fledgling closer relationship with her mother and stepfather.

Beatrice was in her element planning a wedding for her daughter to a prince. A cynical part of Chanel couldn't help wondering how much of her mother's newfound approval stemmed from this unexpected turn of events.

Perry wasn't nearly as overtly critical as he had been in the past, but he didn't go out of his way to extend even pseudo fatherly warmth, either.

As they had been for the majority of her life, Laura and Andrew were two bright beacons of sincere love and affection for Chanel. Their steady presence reminded her that no matter how her life might change by marrying royalty, some things—the truly important things—remained.

Though she saw little of him during the day, Demyan arrived in her room every night— sometimes very late and clearly exhausted. Apparently when he was in Volyarus, his duties extended beyond the company business into the family business: the politics of royalty.

Sometimes they didn't make love before falling into exhausted slumber, but those nights he woke her in the wee hours in order to bring amazing pleasure to her body.

He'd found time to sit with her today, though, while she and her stepfather's lawyer went over the prenuptial agreement. Perry had offered his expertise as well, but honestly?

Chanel trusted Demyan to watch out for her best interests more than her stepfather.

Once she'd read it through, though, she didn't think she needed anyone else's interpretation. For a legal document, the language was straightforward and to the point.

There was some serious overkill in her opinion, but nothing that bothered Chanel to sign.

Upon her marriage, she and her heirs gave up any and all rights they might have in Volyarus, its financial and political endeavors and anything specifically related to the business enterprises of the Yurkovich family.

The fact that particular paragraph was followed by one giving any children she had with Demyan full interest as *his* heirs, she felt was particular overkill.

Clearly, the royal family was very protective of their interests, though. King Fedir's influence, no doubt.

The man had not warmed up to her at all, but he'd never been unkind, either. After her years with Beatrice and Perry, Chanel was practically inured to anything less than overt hostility.

Even with what she was sure were the king's stipulations, the terms of the agreement were very generous toward Chanel, considering the fact she wasn't bringing any significant accumulated wealth to the marriage. The agreement guaranteed an annual sum for living expenses that Chanel couldn't imagine spending in five years, never mind one.

Unless it was on research, but she didn't see Demyan approving using their personal finances to fund her scientific obsessions. Yurkovich Tanner had been generous in that regard already.

One thing the prenup spelled out in black and white, oversize and bolded print to her heart was that Demyan wanted their relationship to be permanent. If she'd been in any doubt.

Which she wasn't.

The financial provision did not decrease in

the event of his death. The annual income was Chanel's and her children's for her lifetime and theirs.

There were some other pretty stringent requirements that would insure she didn't divorce Demyan or be unfaithful to him, though. Not that she would ever do either.

But the agreement spelled out quite clearly that any children born of a different father had absolutely no financial interest through her or any other source in the Yurkovich, Zaretsky or Volyarussian wealth.

Oddly, if she divorced Demyan, or he divorced her for anything other than *her* infidelity, she would still be well taken care of. Until she remarried. If she were ever to marry someone else, or have irrefutable evidence of infidelity brought against her, she lost all financial benefits from her marriage to Demyan.

It wasn't anything less than she expected, but having it spelled out in black and white sent a shiver along her spine that was not exactly pleasant.

Demyan laid his hand over hers before she signed. "You are okay with all the terms?"

"They are more than generous."

"I will always make sure you have what you need, no matter what the agreement says."

"I believe you." And she did. With everything in her.

CHAPTER TEN

THE MORNING OF Chanel's wedding was every bit as tediously focused on beauty, fashion and making an impact as she'd feared it might be with Beatrice in charge.

Strangely, for the first time in her life, Chanel found she didn't mind her mother's fussing over her appearance.

For once, going through the paces of having her legs waxed, her hair done and makeup applied resonated with an almost welcome familiarity in this strange new situation that had become her life.

It had been years since Chanel had sat through one of her mother's preparation routines for a social function, but the sound of Beatrice's voice giving instruction to the stylists resonated with old memories.

Memories were so much easier to deal with

than the reality of the present. She was marrying a prince.

It was beyond surreal.

"Your fingers are like ice." The manicurist frowned as she took Chanel's hand out of the moisturizing soak. "Why did you say nothing? The water must be too cold."

Beatrice was there in a second, testing the water with her own finger and giving Chanel a look filled with concern. "Are you all right, sweetheart?"

Chanel nodded.

Her mom did not look comforted. "The argan oil solution is warm enough, but the manicurist is right. Your hands feel like they've been wrapped around an icicle."

Chanel shrugged.

"Mom, she's marrying a prince. That's not exactly Chanel's dream job," Laura said in that tone only a teenager could get just right. "She's stressed out."

"But he's perfect for you."

"You've barely seen us together. How would you know?" Chanel asked, with little inflection.

"You love him."

Chanel nodded again. There was no point in denying the one thing that would prompt her to marry a man related to royalty.

"He adores you."

Laura grinned at Chanel, her eyes filled with understanding. "I agree with Mom on that one, at least."

"I think he does," Chanel admitted. Demyan acted like a man very happy with his future.

Beatrice reached out and put her hand against Chanel's temple, frowning at whatever she felt there. "You're in shock."

"Sheesh, Mom, way to state the obvious." Laura didn't roll her eyes, but it was close.

Beatrice frowned. "I do not appreciate your tone, young lady."

"Well, you're acting like Chanel should be all excited and happy when it's probably taking everything in her not to run away. She's a scientist, Mom, not a socialite."

"I am well aware of my daughter's chosen profession." Beatrice was careful not to frown—that caused wrinkles—but her tone conveyed displeasure.

The interaction fascinated Chanel, who hadn't

realized her mother and Laura had anything less than the ideal mother-daughter relationship.

Beatrice looked at Chanel. "Do you need some orange juice to bring up your blood sugar?"

Chanel shook her head. "It just doesn't feel real."

"Believe it or not, I threw up twice before walking down the aisle to your father," Beatrice offered with too much embarrassment for it not to be sincere.

Laura snorted. "You were preggers, Mom. It was probably morning sickness."

"I was not morning sick. I was terrified. I nearly fainted when I was getting ready for my wedding to *your* father."

Chanel couldn't imagine her mother agitated to that level. "Really?"

"It's a huge step, marriage. No matter how much you love the man you're marrying."

"I don't know what the big deal is. If it doesn't work out, they can get divorced," Laura said with the blasé confidence of youth.

Their mother glared at her youngest daughter. "That is not the attitude women of this family take into marriage."

"You and Chanel can get all stressed about it, but I'm not going to. If I get married at all. It all seems like a lot of bother over something that ends in divorce about fifty percent of the time. I think living together makes a lot more sense."

Chanel almost laughed at the look of absolute horror crossing their mother's features. She would have, if she could feel anything that deeply.

Right now the entire world around her was one level removed.

"Stop looking like that, Mom. You and Chanel take everything so seriously. I'm not like you."

It was a total revelation to Chanel that Laura considered her like their mother.

"You're more like us than you realize, young lady. Regardless, there will be no more talk of divorce on your sister's wedding day."

Chanel had never heard her mother use that particular tone with her golden-child sister.

And Laura listened, but her less-than-subdued expression implied she *had* heard it before and didn't find it all that intimidating.

How much had Chanel missed about the world around her? She hadn't realized Demyan was a corporate king, much less a real-life prince. She'd had no idea her mother still loved her father and she'd been sure Beatrice no longer loved *her*.

Chanel had been wrong on all counts.

It was a sobering and hopeful realization at the same time.

Nevertheless, she continued through the rest of her personal preparations for the wedding in the fog of shock that had plagued her since waking without Demyan in her bed.

As the makeup artist finished the final application of lip color, a knock sounded at the door.

"The driver is here. Are you both ready?" Beatrice asked, managing to the look the part of the mother of the bride for a prince, anyway.

Laura looked like a blond angel in her ice-blue Vera Wang maid-of-honor dress that was a perfect complement to Chanel's vintage designer gown.

Chanel hoped her mother had worked some kind of magic and she looked her part, as well. She hadn't looked in the mirror since the hair stylist had shown up.

"It's not the driver," Laura announced after

opening the door. Then she dropped into a curtsy and Chanel's throat constricted.

Had the king come to tell her he didn't want Chanel marrying his quasi-adopted son? No, that was an irrational thought.

But...her thoughts stopped their spin out of control in the face of the majesty that was Queen Oxana in full regalia. The Queen of Volyarus swept into the room, making the huge chamber feel very small all of a sudden.

"Good morning, Chanel. Beatrice." The queen gave Chanel's mother a small incline of her head and then a smile to Laura. "Laura, you look lovely."

"Thank you, Your Majesty," Laura replied with her irrepressible smile.

"And you, my dear," the queen said as she focused her considerable attention on Chanel. "You look absolutely perfect. That's an original by Coco Chanel herself, is it not?"

"Yes."

"She was a brilliant and innovative designer who changed the face of female haute couture almost single-handedly. I find your choice to dress in one of her gowns singularly appropri-

ate as I am sure you will be equally as impact-
ing in your field."

It was the first time anyone who mattered to
Chanel emotionally had made such a claim. Bit-
tersweet joy squeezed at her heart, even through
the layer of numbness surrounding that organ.
"Thank you."

Oxana smiled. "You are very welcome." She
offered Chanel a medium-sized dark blue vel-
vet box meant for jewelry. "I would be honored
if you would wear this."

Expecting pearls, or something of that nature, Chanel felt her heart beat in a rapid tattoo
of shock at the sight of the diamond-encrusted
tiara. It wasn't anything as imposing as the
crown presently resting on the queen's perfectly
coiffed hair, but it *was* worthy of a princess.

"I'm not… This is…" Chanel didn't know what
to say, so she closed her mouth on more empty
words.

"Part of my own wedding outfit," the queen
finished for her. "It would please me to see it
worn again."

"Didn't Prince Maksim's wife wear it?" Laura

asked, managing to verbalize at least one of the questions swirling through Chanel's brain.

"King Fedir gave her his mother's princess tiara. It was decided between us that mine would be reserved for the wife of our eldest."

Chanel's heart warmed to hear Demyan referred to as the eldest child of the king and queen.

Somehow, though the stylist had been unaware that a tiara would be added later, the updo she had designed for Chanel lent itself perfectly to the diamond-encrusted accessory.

Or so her mother told Chanel.

"Here, see for yourself," Oxana insisted.

Both Laura and Beatrice gave her a concerned look. So, they had noticed she hadn't looked in the mirror since that morning.

But Chanel didn't want visual proof that she didn't look like a princess.

"I trust your judgment," Chanel hedged.

"Then you will trust my instruction to look at yourself, my soon-to-be daughter." Oxana's expression did not invite argument.

Oh, gosh...she'd never even considered this

woman would truly consider herself Chanel's mother-in-law.

"You look like a princess," Beatrice said with far more sincerity than such a trite statement deserved.

"You're going to knock Demyan on his butt," Laura added with a little less finesse, but no less certainty.

Far from offended, the queen laughed and agreed. "Yes, I do believe you will."

Taking a breath for courage, Chanel turned to face the impartial judge that could not be gainsaid. The mirror reflected only what was—it made no judgments about that image.

The woman staring back at Chanel with wide gray eyes did not look like a queen. No layers and layers of organza to look like any princess bride Chanel had ever seen in the tabloids, either, but in this moment she *was* beautiful.

The vintage Coco Chanel design fit her like it had been tailored to her figure, the antique lace clinging in all the right places. The single-layer floor-length veil and tiara added elegance Chanel was not used to seeing when she looked in a mirror.

The makeup artist had managed to bring out the shape and pink tint of Chanel's lips while making her eyes glow. Her curls had been tamed into perfect corkscrews and then pinned up so that the length of her neck looked almost swan-like.

This woman would not embarrass Demyan walking up the aisle.

Chanel turned to her mother and hugged Beatrice with more emotion than she'd allowed herself to show in years with the older woman. "Thank you."

"It was my pleasure. It has been a very long time since you allowed me to fuss over you. I enjoyed it." Beatrice returned the embrace and then stepped back, blinking at the moisture in her eyes.

Chanel and her mother would probably never agree on what it meant to *fuss* over someone else, but she began to see that, in her own way, her mother hadn't abandoned Chanel completely as a child.

Wearing the gold-and-dark-blue official uniform of the Volyarussian Cossack Hetman, Demyan waited at the bottom of the palace steps, as it was his country's royal tradition that he ride with Chanel in the horse-drawn carriage to the cathedral.

His dark eyes met hers, his handsome face stern and unemotional. Yet despite wearing what she'd come to think of as his "corporate king" face, there was an unmistakable soul-deep satisfaction glimmering in his gaze.

He put his hand out toward her. The white-glove-covered appendage hung there, an unexpected beacon. He wasn't supposed to take her hand yet; he wasn't supposed to touch her at all. They had been instructed to enter the carriage separately. She was to sit with her back toward the driver and he was to face the people on the slow procession to the Orthodox cathedral.

According to the wedding coordinator and royal tradition, she and Demyan were not supposed to touch so much as fingertips until the priest proclaimed them man and wife.

So this one gesture spoke volumes of her prince's willingness to put Chanel ahead of protocol.

Without warning, the mental and emotional fog

surrounding Chanel fell away, the world coming into stark relief for the first time that day. Though it was early fall, the sun shone bright in the sky, the air around them crisp with autumn chill and filled with a cacophony of voices from the crowds lining the palace drive that were suddenly loud.

Love for Demyan swelled inside Chanel, pushing aside worry and doubt to fill her with a certainty that drove her forward toward the hand held out to her.

Their fingers touched, his curling possessively and decisively around her cold ones. He tugged her forward even as electric current arced between them despite the barrier of his glove.

Devastating emotion shuddered through her, completely dispelling the last of the strange, surreal sensations that had plagued her since waking.

His eyes flared and then he was pulling off the cape from his uniform and wrapping it around her. Several gasps sounded around them and the king said something that Chanel had no doubt was a protest.

She couldn't hear him, though, not over the

blood rushing in her ears. The long military cloak settled around her shoulders. She didn't argue that she wasn't really cold, because it carried the fragrance of Demyan's cologne and skin, making her feel embraced by him.

He helped her into the open landau carriage, further eschewing protocol to sit beside her.

Cameras flashed, people cheered and while all of it registered, none of it really impacted Chanel. She was too focused on the man holding her hand and looking at her with quietly banked joy.

"It's just you and me," she said softly, understanding at last.

"Yes."

He didn't relate to her as a prince, though he was undeniably that. Demyan related to her as the man who wanted to share his life with her.

That life might be more complicated because of his title, but at the core, it was the life she wanted. Just as at the core, she knew this man and connected to him soul to soul.

The deep happiness reflecting in his gaze darkened to something more serious. "Always believe that, no matter what else might come up, our marriage is about you and me. Full stop."

"Period," she finished, her heart filled to bursting with such love for this man.

It didn't have to make sense, or be rational, she realized. She had fallen for him immediately and she was wholly and completely *in love* with him now.

They could have waited another year to marry and she wouldn't be any surer of him than she was right now.

As her mom had said, this man was *it* for Chanel, the love of her life, and he felt the same. Even if he hadn't said the words.

Even if he never did.

"I love you," she said to him, needing to in that moment as much as she needed to breathe.

"I will treasure that gift for the rest of my life, I promise you."

He made the vow official less than an hour later when he said it in front of the filled-to-capacity cathedral as part of the personal vows they'd agreed to speak. He also promised to care for her, respect her and support her efforts to make the world a better place through science.

Chanel, who never cried, felt hot tears tracking down her cheeks—thank goodness for her mother's insistence on waterproof makeup—as she spoke her own personal promises, including one to love Demyan for the rest of her life.

It wasn't hard to promise something she didn't think she had a choice about anyway.

His name change was also acknowledged for the first time publicly during the wedding ceremony, when the Orthodox priest led them in their formalized vows before pronouncing them married.

A murmur rippled through the crowd, but Demyan seemed oblivious, his attention wholly on Chanel.

The king's expression was filled with more emotion than Chanel thought the rather standoffish King of Volyarus capable of as he made his official acknowledgment of his *son's* new married state.

Crown Prince Maksim and his wife were both gracious and clearly happy about the name change when Chanel finally met them for the reception line after the ceremony.

She'd thought it odd she hadn't yet met Demyan's *brother* and was relieved when Princess Gillian remarked on it, as well.

It had been clear from several remarks Demyan made that the two men were close. The fact Chanel hadn't been introduced before had had her wondering if maybe the Crown Prince had disapproved of the wedding.

Only now it was obvious he hadn't even known about the upcoming nuptials until he'd been summoned back to Volyarus by his parents. Chanel didn't understand it, but she was the first person to admit that most politics of social interaction and even family relationships went right over her head.

Prince Maksim seemed nice enough and quite willing to accept Chanel into the family. His own wife wasn't royalty or even nobility, so he had to have a fully modern view of marriage within his family.

Though a comment, or two, made by his wife implied otherwise.

Once they'd finished greeting those allowed into the formal reception line, the entire Yurkovich family addressed the people of Volyarus from the main balcony at the front of the palace. The king gave a speech. They all waved and smiled for what felt like hours before everyone but she and Demyan retreated inside.

He addressed the crowd, telling them how honored he was that Dame Chanel Tanner had agreed to be his wife, that he knew her ancestor Baron Tanner would have been very happy, as well.

Then he kissed Chanel.

And it wasn't a chaste, for-the-masses kiss. Demyan took her mouth with gentle implacability, showing her and everyone watching how very pleased he was she was now officially *his*.

Chanel found herself separated from Demyan during the reception, but she wasn't surprised.

He'd prepared her for the way the formal event would unfold, during which they would have very little time together. He had promised to make up for that on their wedding night and the extended honeymoon that was to follow.

What did surprise Chanel was to find herself completely without any of the people who had seemed intent on making sure she was never on her own in the highly political gathering.

Queen Oxana was occupied talking to Princess Gillian. Chanel's mother had been waylaid by an elderly duke, while Andrew flirted with the man's granddaughter under the watchful and not-very-happy gaze of the teen's eagle-eyed mother. Perry was talking business in a corner somewhere—not that he was one of Chanel's self-appointed minders.

Even Laura had lost herself in the crowd.

Chanel thought now would be the ideal time to find a quiet place to regroup a little. The crush of people was overwhelming for a scientist who spent most of her days in the lab, the mixture of so many voices sounding like a roar in her ears.

Seeing a likely hallway, she ducked out of the huge ballroom. The farther she walked along the hallway, the more muted the cacophony of voices from the ballroom became and the more tension drained from her until even her hands, which had been fisted unconsciously at her sides, uncurled.

Only as her fingers straightened did she realize how very hard she'd been holding them.

She could hear voices ahead, one whose tones she recognized with a smile. Demyan.

Delighted by the opportunity to see him amidst

the chaos of her wedding day, she quickened her steps, only slowing down when she realized who he was with.

King Fedir.

The one person who intimidated Chanel and brought out her barely resolved and all-too-recent insecurities. There were two other voices as well, a woman and a man.

They were all speaking Ukrainian, thinly veiled anger resonating in at least two of the speakers' tones.

As Chanel slowed her progress, their conversation resolved itself into actual words she could understand.

The unknown woman demanded, "How dare you humiliate us this way?"

"My actions were not intended as an insult toward you." Demyan did not sound particularly worried the woman had taken whatever he'd done as such, though.

"How could they be taken any other way?" a man who was not the king said. "You have repudiated us before all of Volyarus."

"I didn't repudiate you. I aligned myself with my true family."

"I gave you birth," the woman said in fury.

And the identity of the other two people became clear to Chanel: Demyan's birth parents.

"You also *gave* me to your brother, abdicating any responsibilities and all emotional connections to me. I am no longer your son."

"You are not a child." The man speaking had to be Demyan's biological father. "You know why that was necessary."

"I know that you traded your son for the chance at leverage over your brother-in-law, the king. I know that Fedir and Oxana needed a secondary heir to the throne, but they have always treated me as more than an expedience."

"I'm very pleased you took our house's name, Demyan," the king said with sincerity. "Your parents could have avoided this surprise today by allowing Oxana and me to adopt you as a child. It was their choice not to, as you said... for their own expedience. I, for one, was joyfully surprised and I know your mother feels the same."

Chanel smiled, pleased the outwardly cold man so obviously cared about his adopted son. Demyan said something she did not catch.

"You think you are more than an expedience to the king and queen?" Duke Zaretsky sneered. "He has just ensured you sacrificed the rest of your life for the sake of his family's wealth. You are far more his tool than you were ever mine."

Chanel didn't understand what the duke meant by his words, but there was no question they were intended to wound. And she wasn't about to stand by while anyone tried to hurt Demyan.

She pushed open the door to what turned out to be a very impressive masculine study and crossed to Demyan's side quickly.

His dark gaze flared with something that looked like worry before pleasure at her presence sparked to life, as well. "Hello, *sérdeńko*."

"What are you doing here?" the king asked with his usual less-than-warm attitude toward her.

"The reception was getting too loud."

"You cannot abandon your responsibilities as a hostess on a whim."

"Really? Then what are you doing back here?" she asked with enough sarcasm to be mistaken for her sister. "Correct me if I'm wrong, but wasn't it *your* name on the invitation listed as host of this party?"

Demyan laughed, taking her hand and pulling her to his side. "You make an excellent case, little one."

Everyone in the room except Chanel showed differing levels of surprise at his humor. The king recovered first, giving her a grudging look of respect when she'd expected a frown and polite dressing-down.

She had a lot of experience with both and a lifetime realizing she was no good at taking the path of least resistance, even if it meant avoiding them.

"Point taken," King Fedir said. "We should *all* be getting back."

"Does she know yet?" the duke asked, his expression calculating, his tone undeniably malicious.

CHAPTER ELEVEN

CHANEL DIDN'T ASK what he meant, or even acknowledge the man had spoken.

He'd done it in Ukrainian. Somehow she
doubted Demyan had been into sharing con-
fidences with the older man, which meant the
duke had no idea she understood the language.
That made his choice to converse in it pointedly
without courtesy.

"You will be silent," the king replied in the
same language to his brother-in-law, his tone
harsh.

Ignoring both posturing men, Chanel smiled
up at Demyan. "I missed you."

"Oh, how sweet," Princess Svitlana said in a
tone that made it clear she thought it was anything but.

Demyan's expression was an odd mixture of
tenderness and a strange underlying anxiety as
he looked down at Chanel. "I am very proud of

you. Not many science geeks would do so well at an affair of state with so little training."

"You assigned a very potent group of baby-sitters."

His nostrils flared as if her words surprised him.

"You didn't think I realized you'd asked them to watch over me?" Once she had, she'd felt very well cared for.

Demyan would never leave Chanel to sink or swim in the shark-infested waters of his life.

"I could not be with you the entire time," he said by way of an explanation.

Not that she'd needed one. "Because you're a prince."

"It's a nominative title only," his birth mother said with more venom, in English this time. "He's no more a prince than you are a well-bred princess."

Chanel gave the older woman a measure of her attention, but kept her body and clear allegiance toward Demyan. "I am not a horse and I wasn't born in a breeding program. While I won't claim to be a princess, Demyan is definitely a prince."

"He won't inherit. Not now that Princess Gillian is carrying the next heir to the throne."

"But he is the king and queen's son. That makes him a prince."

"I gave birth to him," the duchess said.

Chanel found it odd that the duke never verbalized his claim at fatherhood. "Congratulations."

"Are you mocking me?"

"No. I don't know what your other children are like. Hopefully more like their older brother than their parents, but I do know you gave birth to an amazing man in Demyan. I'm sure you are very proud of that accomplishment, but you aren't his mother any more than I am a princess."

"Oxana is my mother," Demyan asserted with absolute assurance.

"And you would do anything for her and the man you consider your father, even marry some socially backward American *scientist* to protect the Yurkovich financial interests." She said scientist as if it was a dirty word.

Chanel almost smiled. She'd never considered her vocation as beyond the pale before.

"That is enough, Svitlana." The king's tone was again harsh, his expression forbidding.

"Oh, so you *haven't* told her?" Duke Zaretsky asked snidely, clearly ignoring his king's evident wrath and this time taking evident pleasure in speaking English. "I could almost feel sorry for her. She gave up hundreds of millions of dollars by marrying you and she doesn't even know it."

There could be no doubt the duke was talking about Chanel, but the words made absolutely no sense.

"I didn't give up anything and gained everything marrying Demyan," she fiercely asserted.

The duchess looked at her pityingly. "You have no idea, but no matter what kind of prenuptial agreement these two convinced you to sign, until you spoke your vows three hours ago, you were a twenty-percent owner in Yurkovich Tanner."

"I wasn't. My great-great-grandfather left his shares to the Volyarussian people." He'd told her great-grandmother so in a letter still in Chanel's possession, along with the family Bible.

"And they have been used to finance infrastructure, schools and hospitals since then," the king assured her.

She smiled at him, holding no grudge for his unwelcoming demeanor. "I know. I did some research when I got the scholarship. Your country is kind of amazing for its progressive stance on the environment and energy conservation."

"I am glad you think so."

"That money was yours," the king's sister insisted. "Until you married my son."

The claims were starting to make an awful kind of sense, but Chanel had no intention of allowing the two emotional vultures in front of her to know about the splinters of pain slicing their way through Chanel's heart.

She simply said, "He's not your son."

"Would you like to see your grandfather's will?" the duke asked, clearly unwilling to give up.

Two things were obvious in that moment. The first was that there had to be some truth to what the duke and his wife were saying. If there wasn't, Demyan and the king would have categorically denied it.

Also, they were both way too tense now for the claims to be entirely false.

Second, whatever the duke and Princess Svitlana's motives for telling Chanel, it had nothing to do with helping or protecting *anyone*. Her least of all.

In fact, she was fairly certain their intention was to hurt the son who had finally made a public alliance with the family who had raised him.

She turned away from the duke and duchess to face Demyan. "Tell me your siblings don't take after your egg and sperm donors."

Duplicate sounds of outrage indicated the Zaretskys had heard her just fine.

Demyan didn't respond, an expression she'd never seen in his eyes. Fear.

She wasn't sure what he was afraid of. Whether he was afraid she would mess up whatever plan he'd made with King Fedir, or worried she would go ballistic at their very politically attended reception, or something else really didn't matter.

Whatever Demyan felt for her, Chanel loved him and she wasn't going to let the two people whose rejection had already caused him a lifetime of pain hurt him anymore.

"I think it's time we all returned to the reception." She couldn't quite dredge up a smile, but she did her best to mask her own hurt.

He spoke then, the words coming out in a strange tone. "We need to talk."

She didn't want him showing vulnerability

in front of the Zaretskys. Chanel wasn't giving them the satisfaction of believing they'd succeeded in their petty and vindictive efforts.

She reached up and cupped his face, like he did so often with her, hoping it gave him the same sense of comfort and being cared for it had always done her, no matter how much of a lie it might have been at the time. "Later."

"You promise?"

"Yes."

"She is a fool," the duke said in disgusted Ukrainian.

Chanel looked at him over her shoulder, her expression a perfect reflection of her mother's favorite one for disdain. "The only fool here is you if you think for one second you have the power to influence my prince's life for good or ill today, or any time in the future. You simply don't matter."

She had also spoken in his native language and enjoyed the shock that produced in the overweening nobleman.

The duchess gasped. "You're American."

"Which does not equate to uninformed, stupid or uneducated." Chanel met eyes so similar in color but different in expression from Demyan's. "My heritage in this country may not be royal, or as long-standing, but when it comes to the welfare of Volyarus, it is equally as important as yours."

Her grandfather had helped this nation stay afloat financially three decades ago and his efforts were still benefitting the Volyarussians.

"You already knew," the duchess said, almost as if she admired Chanel's acumen. "But then why did you marry him?"

"Because she loves me," Demyan said, his voice gravelly.

Chanel turned back to him without agreeing or giving his parents another single solitary moment of her time. She hadn't known about the will being different than what her great-grandmother had believed, or what that had to do with Chanel's marriage to Demyan, though she could make a pretty educated guess based on the prenuptial agreement.

She wasn't about to admit that to the Zaretskys, though.

Demyan was searching her face as if trying to read Chanel's thoughts. So far in their relationship, she'd been an open book. She had little hope of hiding what was going on in her head right now.

But she didn't have to talk about it. Especially in front of the older generation of the royal family.

"Leave," the king said to his sister and brother-in-law.

The Zaretskys started for the door of the study.

"No," the king instructed. "Out through the secret passage. You will not return to the reception and you will be out of the palace within the hour."

"What? You cannot be serious. How would that look?" his sister demanded.

"Like you threw a temper tantrum when your son chose to change his name to reflect his true parentage," the king replied, his tone arctic.

Princess Svitlana crossed her arms, but stopped just shy of stomping her feet. "I won't do it."

"You will. Do not presume to forget that this is not a nominal King of Volyarus. I hold the power to revoke your citizenship and deport you. Do not tempt me to use it."

The duke and his wife both paled at the king's

words, Princess Svitlana doing a fair imitation of a gasping fish, though no words passed her lips.

The expression in her brother's eyes suggested she keep it that way.

Showing she was marginally more intelligent than evidence might suggest, the princess left without another word. Through the secret passageway. Her husband followed close behind her.

Chanel stepped back from Demyan, intending to return to the reception. The crowds of people and litany of voices that fifteen minutes ago had seemed so overwhelming now called like a beacon for escape from the thoughts that were multiplying by the second in her head.

And with every new thought came a shard of pain Chanel had no idea how long she could contain.

The king blocked her exit, his gaze searching hers as much as his adopted son's had done. However, the level of ruthlessness behind his perusal chilled her; she'd felt only confusion mixed with hurt at Demyan's look.

She said nothing, simply waited for the King of Volyarus to move.

He frowned. "You will not return to the reception only to cause a scene."

She was doing her best to hold back an emotional devastation she hadn't experienced since her father's death. Did he really think his display of bossiness was helping the situation?

"Let me give you a small piece of advice, Your Majesty."

His brows rose in obvious shock at her tone.

She went on, "Right this second, all I see when I look at you is a man who would use whatever underhanded means are necessary to rob a woman and her family of a legacy they knew nothing about."

"There was nothing underhanded about your marriage to my son. It is legal in every sense. You cannot undo it."

She said a word that rarely passed her lips, but called the lie for what it was. Oh, he might be correct in that she could not undo whatever legality the wedding had wrought, but as for nothing about it being devious?

That was an ugly bit of nonsense. "All I've done so far is tell you my opinion, not offered my advice. If you're smart, you will take it."

"Chanel, you cannot speak to him like that," Demyan said, sounding tired rather than corrective. "He is your king."

"Not *my* king." Any more than Demyan was *her* prince.

King Fedir asked before Demyan could reply to that claim, "What is your advice?"

"Do not attempt to tell me what to do. Because though my intention is *not* to embarrass my family, or Queen Oxana who has been nothing but kind to me, your very instruction not to cause a scene is nearly overwhelming impetus to do so."

"You love my son."

She didn't deny it. What would be the point? Everyone in that room knew the truth about her emotions. And his now, no matter how misled she'd been that morning.

"But I don't even like you," she told Demyan's adopted father very succinctly.

The king flinched, his face slackening in shock as if he'd never had anyone speak to him in such a way before. Maybe he hadn't.

"Chanel…" That was Demyan, the tone in his voice not one she wanted to hear or could even begin to trust right then.

Definitely not admonishment for her rudeness to his father, but what it was, she refused to name.

She spun to face him, her heart in a vise that brought pain with each indrawn breath. "Don't. Just *don't,* Demyan. However horrible their intentions, the duke and duchess were more honest with me than you've been."

"No." He lurched forward, as if he'd been yanked by a string attached to his chest.

She stepped back quickly, sure of one thing. She could not allow him to touch her right now. "Stop. I said later. I meant *later.*"

"Perhaps you two should speak *now,*" the king said, sounding less certain than he had to this point.

Chanel made no attempt to hide the utter dislike she felt when she faced him. "You're doing it again. You say maybe we should talk and all I can think is how much more certain I am that there isn't going to be any more talking."

"You are a contrary woman."

"You have no idea how contrary I can be, but spend a few minutes talking with my stepfather and he'll fill you in."

"I have spent some time in his company already."

And heard an earful, Chanel was sure. For the first time in her life, she simply didn't care if Perry had managed to turn someone right off her. "I'm sure he enjoyed that."

"He's an opportunistic man."

"He is." Something clicked in her mind, two memories coming together to form a single conclusion. "He's the one, isn't he, the reason you had to act now?"

The king's face smoothed over into an emotionless mask, but not before she saw the flare of surprise at her guess.

Because she was right.

"My great-great-grandfather Tanner died, apparently with a very different will to the one my great-grandmother believed to have been in existence. Yet no one from your family has approached mine in four generations to secure Baron Tanner's shares in your precious company."

"It is not just a company—it is the financial cornerstone of an entire country."

"Your country."

"Yours now, too."

"That remains to be seen."

"Chanel—" Demyan tried to say something.

She put her hand up. "No. Not you. Not now. Trust me when I tell you it is better for everyone if you show that ruthless patience you are so well-known for in business."

"How do you know about that?"

"I've spent six weeks learning you." Too bad he hadn't done the same.

He would have realized there was no worse way she could have learned of his subterfuge than to be told by an outside party. But then maybe he had realized and it simply didn't matter.

He wouldn't risk upsetting whatever scheme he and his father had set in motion to protect their precious wealth and thereby their country.

She focused on the king again. "My stepfather approached your company trying to trade on connections he didn't really have, but it got you all worried."

"He is a resourceful man."

"He's a shark, though I think maybe Demyan is a bigger, and much meaner, one."

"Without doubt." The king sounded proud.

But then he would be, wouldn't he? His son's ruthless resourcefulness had netted him full interest in Yurkovich Tanner for the first time in four generations.

She didn't know how, or what the details were, but that much she had gleaned from what had and had not been said in this room tonight.

"There are half-a-dozen moderately accessible chemical compounds that would eat the flesh from a shark's body in less than a minute, did you know that?"

The king shook his head, his expression almost bemused.

"I did. I know every single one of them."

"Are you threatening him?"

"I am reminding you that even sharks get eaten if they aren't careful and it doesn't always take a bigger shark to do it."

"I believe there is a strand of ruthlessness in you, too."

"Would you like to find out?"

The king opened his mouth and then closed it, giving Demyan a look of concern before his expression turned thoughtful. "No."

"Good."

"What do you plan to do?"

"Throw the bouquet."

"You know that is not what I meant."

"I care?"

The king's mouth tightened, but he stepped aside, having seemingly finally gotten the message that his admonitions were more effective goads to bad behavior than preventers of it.

Chanel threw the bouquet.

She even managed to dredge up a photo-op-worthy smile when Laura caught it and tossed it away again immediately. Her sister's attitude toward the institution of marriage couldn't have been more obvious.

Chanel had to wonder if the teenager had caught the bouquet just so she could throw it away again. The entire ballroom erupted into laughter and even Beatrice was smiling.

She should be.

Her disappointment of a daughter had managed to land a prince. No wonder she'd come to Chanel's apartment with stories of undying first love.

Chanel couldn't believe she'd thought her mom was finally showing a vested interest in her oldest daughter's happiness.

But then she'd let herself be convinced that Demyan *wanted* to marry *her.* Not Bartholomew Tanner's only surviving heir.

Smile still fixed firmly in place, Chanel looked out over the ballroom full of people. Her gaze settled on Queen Oxana. The older woman looked pleased, her normally controlled expression filled with unmistakable happiness.

Was that because she knew the Yurkovich fortune was secure, or was she happy at what she thought was her son's marriage to someone she believed was his one true love?

Another memory clicked into place and the smile fell away from Chanel's face. Oxana was the one who had made Demyan promise not to use protestations of love to convince Chanel to marry him.

The queen knew about the will. She must, but she had scruples where her husband and son did not. She might be the only person Chanel could trust to tell her the truth.

She was tempted to leave the reception early, but every time she let her gaze find Demyan, he was watching her. He would only follow her, but she wanted a chance to talk to his mother, to get some answers on her own first.

She got her chance unexpectedly when Oxana came up to her and laid a hand on her arm. "Are you all right, Chanel?"

Chanel looked toward Demyan. He returned her regard, his dark-eyed expression unreadable, but something in the way he watched Chanel and his mother told Chanel he had sent the older woman to her.

"You know," Chanel said instead of answering.

"That you and my husband had something of an altercation earlier? Yes."

Interesting that the queen considered the argument to be between Chanel and the king, not Chanel and Demyan. "Did he tell you?"

"Demyan did."

Even the sound of his name on Oxana's lips hurt Chanel in some indefinable way. "You were aware of their plans because of my great-great-grandfather's will."

Oxana nodded.

"You made him promise not to lie about loving me. Thank you." She wasn't sure how much worse the pain inside her would be if she'd believed false words of love. "I want to read the will."

"If you ask Demyan, he will tell you everything."

"I don't want to hear from him. He had his chance to tell me. He chose not to."

"He was trying to protect our nation."

Chanel couldn't help mocking. "Because I'm such a huge security risk."

Oxana looked around them, obviously concerned someone might overhear. No one was in range of their subdued tones, but that could change any second.

"I don't want to be here," Chanel admitted hopelessly.

There was nowhere else she could be without someone she didn't want to talk to following her, which included pretty much everyone but Oxana at the moment.

The queen sighed, looking at her sadly. "He cares for you."

Maybe Oxana wouldn't be the best company either. Chanel just shook her head, moving to turn away.

But Oxana's hand on her arm stopped her from putting distance between them. "Come, I will take you someplace away from the scrutiny and company of others."

Chanel thought it a bit obvious when the queen led her to the retiring room for the ladies, but they didn't stop in the outer room as she expected. The queen led her into one of the three small chambers with toilets, closing the door behind them.

While the room was larger than the usual commode stall, it wasn't exactly meant for two people and Chanel didn't think talking about sensitive subjects with only a door between them and anyone who walked into the lounge was a good idea.

But Oxana did not ask any questions, or make any attempts at comfort. She simply pushed up on a section of wainscoting and then the wall behind the commode swung backward.

Oxana put her hand out to Chanel. "Come, I'll

take you to the private papers library for the House of Yurkovich. Your great-great-grandfather's will has been stored there."

CHAPTER TWELVE

Darkness surrounded Chanel as she stood on the balcony overlooking the now-silent grounds of the palace. The reception was long over, the last guest's car having left the drive thirty minutes before.

Temperatures had dropped since that morning and she shivered in the cold air, but she did not go back inside.

Before leaving her to read over the will and relevant places in Bartholomew Tanner's diaries the queen had marked for Chanel, Oxana had told her that her favorite place for solitude was this balcony.

"The bedrooms do not have security cameras in them, but they do have infrared monitoring. The public rooms and hallways are all covered with video feed, though. The only two places in the palace where you can relax unmonitored in any way are the public address balcony and the one outside Fedir's rooms."

"Isn't that a security risk?" Chanel had asked.

But Oxana had shaken her head. "The walls and every approach are covered."

Which meant that Demyan would eventually find her because Chanel's path to the balcony would have been tracked by video monitoring once she left the secret passageway.

She could have left the palace completely. Chanel was a resourceful woman and there had been dozens of cars departing the grounds over the past few hours.

But she wasn't a coward and she'd never hidden from the truth, no matter how much it might hurt to face.

What that truth was, however, wasn't entirely clear. Not after reading the will. Not after remembering Demyan's words in the carriage that morning.

Not after having Oxana tell Chanel exactly what promise she'd extracted from her son over the *love* thing.

Not until Chanel asked Demyan the only question that really mattered.

"Chanel."

She turned at the sound of her name on Demyan's lips.

He stood framed by the light from the hall. He reached and flipped a switch. More golden light flooded the balcony.

"Turn it off," she said, angling her head away so he could not see the damage tears had done on even the indelible makeup job her mother's professional artist had applied.

"No. We do not need more shadows in our relationship."

She swung back to face him head-on, anger making her muscles rigid with tension. "The shadows are all you."

He nodded, his expression as tortured as she felt, if she could believe the evidence of her eyes.

She wasn't sure she trusted her own perceptions at all, though, not after how easily he'd taken her in. However, she didn't think he could fake the parchment-pale of his complexion, the way his black pupils nearly swallowed the espresso irises or the way he breathed in what she would consider panicked gasps in anyone else.

"That day in my lab. It was planned."

"I needed to meet you. You are not a social person."

"So Yurkovich Tanner donated five million dollars to my department for research. That's an expensive introduction." Though nothing in comparison to what the Yurkovich fortune stood to lose if she had made her claim on the Tanner shares in the company.

"It also ensured you were predisposed to look on me favorably."

"Your idea, or the king's?"

"Does it matter?"

"No."

"You've read the will."

"Oxana told you."

"I saw you go into the personal archives library on the video monitor feedback."

"Oh."

"I spent two hours watching the tapes, trying to find you."

"We used the secret passages."

"Yes. You only showed up for brief periods on the video monitors and there were too many extra people in the palace to track you with the infrared body counter and placement."

"Poor you."

"Cha…" Her name choked off and he stepped forward, stumbling, though she knew the stone floor was smooth with no hindrances.

"You never needed your glasses." For anything.

He stopped a couple of feet from her. "I told you that."

"But I thought you needed them as an emotional crutch."

"I do not use crutches."

"No. A man without emotions doesn't need crutches for them, does he?"

"I am human, damn it, not a puppet. I have emotions."

"I bet it was the king's idea to approach me looking like a corporate geek to match my science-nerd personality."

"He believed I would be too intimidating in my usual way."

"That man, the corporate shark, he's part of you."

"Yes."

"But he's not all of you."

"I thought he was."

"Until when?" she pushed.

"Until I met you."

"You don't mean that."

"I've never meant anything more."

"You lied to me."

"I am ruthless when it comes to protecting my country and those I love."

"I noticed."

"There is little hope that will change."

"No. It's part of your nature. You would have made a very good Cossack."

"We still have the elite in our army. As tradition dictates, I spent two years training with them before going to university."

"Wasn't that Prince Maksim's job?"

"He wasn't the oldest son to the king."

"But he is heir to the throne."

"Yes."

"Does that bother you?"

"No. I hate politics."

"I hate being deceived."

"I will not do it again."

"Can you really promise that, with your ruthless nature?"

"Yes."

"Why?"

"I don't understand."

"I think you do."

If anything, his face paled further. "Don't, Chanel."

"Don't what? Make you admit your vulnerabilities. If you have any, that is."

"I do."

"I'm not stupid by any stretch, you know. Legalese may not be science speak, but I understand it well enough."

"Yes?"

"Yes. Bartholomew Tanner's will is unambiguous. My marriage to you negated all claim I, or any of my children, had to Yurkovich Tanner."

Demyan nodded.

"The prenuptial didn't need to spell that out at all."

"No."

"You had that paragraph added as a kind of warning to me, didn't you?"

He shrugged.

"You also made sure I would be taken care of financially despite the fact that legally I would have no way of pursuing any monetary interests in the future."

"You are my wife. I wanted you provided for."

"I bet the king just loved the terms of the pre-nup."

"He agreed to them."

She was sure there was a story there, but right now she wasn't interested in hearing it. "You came after me with the intention of securing Volyarussian economic stability, no matter the cost."

"Yes." The word sounded torn out of him.

"You could have just asked me to sign the shares over and I would have done it. Especially after reading my grandfather's diaries."

"His diaries?"

"He spelled out his intention of leaving the shares to the people of Volyarus, but at first he was still holding out hope your great-uncle would marry my great-grandmother, then he got his hopes set on the next generation. He died before he could try to make that alliance happen."

"I am aware."

"What you didn't know was that he'd writ-ten my great-grandmother and told her that he planned to leave his interest in Yurkovich Tanner to the Volyarussian people. I never would have tried to undermine his clear wishes."

"Your stepfather would not be so sanguine. He might well have convinced your mother to bring suit on her deceased husband's behalf."

"A suit that wouldn't have gone anywhere without my cooperation, and I wouldn't have given it."

"We did not know that."

"You had to have realized, as you got to know me."

"Once I commit to a purpose, I do not change my direction on a whim or the hope of a different outcome."

"Maybe you decided you *wanted* to marry me." It was hard to say the words, to put it out there like that, but this man was about as in touch with his emotions as the puppet he was so adamant he was not.

"I did want to marry you."

"Why?"

He stared at her, his expression so open she wanted to cry. Because it showed so much that he so clearly didn't know how to express verbally. One thing was really obvious. This man did not know what to do with his emotions.

"We are very compatible."

"Are we?"

"You know we are."

"You're a prince. I'm a scientist."

"Those are our titles, not who we are at the core."

"Okay, then you're ruthless and I'm insecure. We're both emotionally repressed."

"But you are more secure about yourself with me."

"And you are less ruthless with me?" she asked, already knowing the answer.

Looking back on it, she saw that the prenuptial agreement was practically a love letter from Demyan.

The uncertainty in his expression was heartbreaking. "Yes?"

She couldn't hold back from touching him any longer. She stepped right into his personal space and he wrapped his arms around her like it was the most natural thing in the world to do.

"Yes, Demyan. *Yes.*" His ruthlessness wasn't

always a bad thing, but she brought out the best in him, too.

Now, if she could just get him to realize what that meant.

"You turn me on like no other woman ever has." He spoke as if that fact confused him. "I don't like being without you. Not even for a couple of days. It makes it hard to focus."

"I'm glad to hear that. I feel the same way."

"I miss you," he stressed. "Every hour we are apart. Even when I am working."

No matter how this thing between them had started, it had caught Demyan in the whirlwind of emotion right along with her. Which was the conclusion she'd finally come to after a lot of pain-filled soul-searching and examination of every memory from the moment they'd met.

"It hurt finding out about the will and your reason for marrying me from your sperm donor."

Pain twisted Demyan's features. "I am sorry." He reached up to wipe along the tear streaks on one cheek. "You cried."

"At first, all I could think was that you'd tricked me into loving you when you felt nothing for me at all. That you probably planned on getting rid of me as soon as the ink was dry on the marriage certificate."

"No!" He kissed her, the connection between their mouths infused with a desperation stronger than anything she'd ever felt from him.

It was a magnified version of the feelings that emanated off him at night when making love since their arrival in Volyarus.

She did nothing to stop the kiss for a long time, needing this connection as badly as he so clearly did.

But eventually, she broke her mouth away. "Were you going to tell me?"

"Maybe someday. I do not know. I did not want to."

"You were afraid."

"I am never afraid."

"Not usually, but the idea of losing me scared you."

"Have I lost you?" His arms tightened around her even as he asked the question.

"No."

"No?" he asked, his voice breaking so the word sounded as if it had two syllables.

"Definitely not. Yet."

His big body went absolutely rigid. "Yet?"

"It all depends on your answer to a question."

He stared down at her.

"You never break your promises, right?" She let her body mold completely to his, trying to give him strength.

That's what people who loved each other did— they lent their strength when it was needed.

"Right."

"Tell me you love me."

The tension emanating off him increased exponentially.

"Your mom told me what she made you promise her."

Demyan's expression was haunted.

"You promised not to say you love me unless you really mean it," Chanel reminded him. "You can say it now, Demyan. I will treasure your love forever, too."

"But…"

"You love me."

"I do?"

"That stuff you were saying earlier, about missing me, being afraid to lose me, even the way you changed the prenuptial agreement, it all means one thing."

"It does?" Comprehension and acceptance dawned over his features, making him smile with heartbreaking happiness. "It does. I love you, Chanel, more than my life as a prince. More than anything."

More tears filled her eyes, but these didn't burn or hurt her heart. "I love you, too."

"I mean it."

"I know."

"No, I mean…we don't have to live with the whole royalty thing. I know it's not the life you want. I can abdicate my role."

It wasn't an empty promise and it would not come without significant cost to this amazing man. Especially after finally acknowledging his true role as son of Oxana and Fedir, but Demyan was entirely sincere in his offer.

"No. I love you, Demyan. Ruthless prince. Corporate king and shark. All of you."

"I love you for all that you are, too, Chanel, and that includes the woman who has never aspired to be a socialite."

"I'm not going to be one now, either."

"My uncle…father is not going to know what to do with you."

"He'll probably call me princess just to annoy me."

Demyan laughed, the sound freer and filled with more joy than she'd ever heard from him. "You may well be right."

"So long as you call me love."

"*Koxána moja*," he said, calling her his love in Ukrainian. "Always and forever. You are the very heart that beats inside my chest."

And then he took her back to the rooms they would share whenever staying at the palace for the years to come and made tender, night-long love to her, using those words and so many others to tell Chanel that this man truly loved her and always would.

Later she snuggled into his body and yawned as she said, "I guess it's a good thing you've got a sneaky, underhanded side."

"Is it?"

"Yep."

"Why?"

"We never would have gotten together otherwise. You snuck past all my barriers."

"It is only fair, since you destroyed mine."

Two broken people who had not even realized they were broken had been made whole by love.

Yes, Chanel thought, that was exactly right and fair.

"Love you, Demyan."

"I love you."

"Always."

"For the rest of our lives."

"And beyond." Eternity would not end a love so strong.

"And beyond."

EPILOGUE

OXANA CUDDLED HER latest grandchild. The tiny infant was only three days old, but he was so alert that the queen could not help smiling into soft gray eyes so like his mother's.

Little Damon was her fourth grandchild and she had no doubts he would bring her every bit as much joy as the other three she'd been gifted by her sons and their wives.

The oldest, Mikael, was five and the only child Gillian and Maksim had conceived. Their youngest was adopted, a beautiful little girl who had both her besotted parents wrapped around her dainty little fingers.

Demyan and Chanel's oldest had turned two, four months before the birth of her little brother. Both children were cosseted and adored by parents who showed a decided ruthlessness when it came to putting their family first.

Oxana could not be more pleased. She'd given

up a lifetime of love and found little personal happiness in order to give her sons the best chance at a better life. One would be king, the other would continue to oversee their business interests, but both were blissfully happy.

And Oxana thought that a more-than-fair compensation for the sacrifices she'd made. After all, she had her grandchildren around her now. They called her Nana, not Your Majesty, and didn't hesitate to muss her designer couture with messy fingers.

How incredibly blessed she was, but her sons had received the true gift beyond measure.

A lifetime love with women who not only knew but accepted both men for who and what they were.

Fedir often didn't know what to make of his independent-minded daughters by marriage, but he loved being a grandfather and already had grand plans for the children.

Oxana didn't tell him, but she had plans, too, and she knew exactly what each grandchild needed for the future. Love.

Just as she had done her best to make sure both her sons realized their loves, she would do whatever it took to ensure each of her grandchildren knew true love, as well.

Fedir could plan all the machinations he wanted, but in the end? Love would triumph.

Just as it had for her children.

* * * * *

Mills & Boon® Large Print

December 2013

Mills & Boon® Large Print
January 2014

CHALLENGING DANTE
Lynne Graham

CAPTIVATED BY HER INNOCENCE
Kim Lawrence

LOST TO THE DESERT WARRIOR
Sarah Morgan

HIS UNEXPECTED LEGACY
Chantelle Shaw

NEVER SAY NO TO A CAFFARELLI
Melanie Milburne

HIS RING IS NOT ENOUGH
Maisey Yates

A REPUTATION TO UPHOLD
Victoria Parker

BOUND BY A BABY
Kate Hardy

IN THE LINE OF DUTY
Ami Weaver

PATCHWORK FAMILY IN THE OUTBACK
Soraya Lane

THE REBOUND GUY
Fiona Harper